CHERRY PIE OR DIE

A BAKER STREET MYSTERY

CEECEE JAMES

For my Family

CONTENTS

BLURB

After a traumatic life event, Georgie Tanner returns to her hometown to start her life over... at 31 years old. Add a painful memory to the mix and Georgie is a certified hot mess.

Luckily, Aunt Cecelia is there with a job for Georgie. She might not feel able to take on the world, but she thinks she's up for taking tourists through Gainesville, Pennsylvania's historic downtown. The place is as American as apple pie, steeped in rich Revolutionary history, Amish settlements, ghost stories, and colonial manors. Georgie knew it was a safe place to go to piece back her memories.

After all, what could go wrong in a sleepy town like this?

Until she leads a group of tourists through the Three

Maidens' Manor, a battle site converted into a museum. When the power goes out during the tour, Georgie thinks it's a crazy fluke. But when it returns, she has six panicked guests, and a dead man in her midst.

Who would want to kill him? And more importantly, which one of them was the murderer?

This book is a work of fiction and although it does discuss events and places from the American Revolutionary War, the setting of the book is a fictional town utilizing facts from the war in order to enhance the story.

CHAPTER 1

The day was unseasonably warm for autumn, in just the type of way that made me regret wearing my cranberry-colored merino wool sweater. It looked amazing, but it was all I could do to ignore the sweat gathering in my bra. The sweater was one of the last surviving remnants from my dead career as a paralegal at a law firm, and I wore it with a mixture of emotions. Despite the heat, I was stuck wearing it now, with only a silk camisole underneath. I pushed up the sleeves and gripped the steering wheel with sweaty hands.

Usually, early October was known for blustering winds and even an occasional snowfall here in Lancaster County, Pennsylvania. But on my drive this morning, I was surprised to notice a few bright red Cardinal flowers still blooming along the road, competing with the orange and gold leaves.

I drove my repurposed catering van down the bumpy dirt driveway to park in front of the Baker Street Bed and Breakfast, leaving clouds of dust behind me. The van did its usual clunks and shudders before finally turning off.

This was my Aunt Cecelia's business. Well, she wasn't really my aunt, but that's a complicated story. She ran the bed and breakfast out of her home, along with a tour company. Our little town, Gainesville, sat right in the thick of many rich American Revolution historical landmarks. We got an influx of tourists every year wanting help as they explored the area.

That's what made Cecelia's bed and breakfast different. She'd come up with a unique vacation experience that coupled quaint bedrooms and home-cooked meals with a tour that took her guests to all of the best historical sites.

I tucked my short hair around my ear—a new haircut for a new life, and I loved it—and looked at the B&B now. The climbing roses that added so much charm to the front of the house trailed up trellises that bordered each of the front windows. The roses were wild and wispy, and had lost most of their leaves. I wrinkled my nose. It was kind of getting late in the season to prune them back. I needed to find more time to get the chores done, that precious commodity that always had me chasing after it.

We had seven guests staying at the B&B at the moment, and the first two—a married couple—strolled out onto the front porch. They must have been watching for me by the window. Michael and Rachel were their names, although I referred to them as Mr. and Mrs. Green.

Mrs. Green waved and slid on a pair of enormous sunglasses that, even from this distance, I could see held a touch of class.

Something that the used catering van was surely lacking. Still, this van had been the sole bargain the car salesman from Champions used car lot had shown me after our last vehicle threw an engine rod. Only one previous owner, the salesman had claimed, and super low miles! I should have been more suspicious when he added, "Don't worry, the smell will air out." But my wallet was on the slimmer side at the time, so it seemed like a deal to me.

Well, it's true the van had low miles, but the scent of barbecue sauce continued to linger in the air, especially on a hot day like today. I reached into the glove box and spritzed a bit of vanilla air freshener, then rolled down the window and climbed out.

"Hi, there," I said, with my million-watt customer smile, as I walked up the steps. The wood creaked under my leather boots. "How was last night? Did you have a good night's sleep?"

"Hi, Georgie! It was wonderful. So peaceful out here," said Mrs. Green, running perfectly manicured fingers through her long blonde hair. Carefully, she coiled it over one shoulder. She was a young woman, in her late twenties, but dressed in clothing suited to someone much older. Still, she was sophisticated, with her designer shoes and expensive purse.

Her husband was tall, somewhere in his sixties, with hair as white as the first snowfall on the Pocono Mountains. The town didn't have too many May/December residents, but I'd seen a fair number as guests.

"You both ready to go exploring?" I asked as I skirted around them on my way to the front door.

"You better believe we are," Mrs. Green answered. So far she'd been an enthusiastic participant in the last two places we'd gone to. I'd been impressed, dressed as fancy as she was, that she didn't mind delving into some of these dusty buildings and cemeteries. "But you-know-who is dragging her feet again."

Mr. Green chuckled while I bit back a groan. I knew exactly who Mrs. Green was referring too: Eliza Sue Remington, a self-proclaimed spinster in her early forties. That woman dressed as though she thought spinsterhood was her true calling in life, with her brown hair rolled into bobbing curls, elastic-waisted jeans, and blue tennis shoes.

"Well, I'll go check on her then. I'll be right back," I said.

As I reached for the door, it swung open, and a third guest joined us. This was Mr. Peterson, a good-looking single man in his thirties from Boston, who claimed he was a serious history buff. He held an unlit cigarette.

"All ready to go," he said. "Just getting my last cancer stick in."

I smiled. "I'll let everyone know I'm here, and then we can take off."

He lit his cigarette and took a drag. "Good luck with that." He nodded, giving me a wink.

I shook my head and walked inside. There was no doubt that man was a bit of a player, but because he was handsome, he thought he could get away with it.

The inside of the Bed and Breakfast was kept in a vintage style. Cecelia had purchased the home straight after her retirement, and had renovated it carefully to preserve all of its old charm. I could hear her now, singing as she bustled about in the kitchen. Sugary scents of French toast and coffee filled the air. I walked past the dining room and saw that, with the exception of a few coffee cups and a glass of orange juice, breakfast had been cleared.

I entered the living room. Sitting on the couch, with bored

expressions pasted to their faces, were the St. Claires. They were the other married couple, somewhere in their early forties, and were celebrating their wedding anniversary. They'd shared with me how they'd already been to Florida and South Carolina, and that Pennsylvania was their last hurrah before returning home.

"We first met down in Florida," Mrs. St. Claire had told me. "Out on the beach. Jared saw me and couldn't wait to get me into his home. Va Va Va Voom!"

It seemed by his countenance now that Mr. St. Claire was quite ready for his home once again. His head was propped on his upright arm that leaned against the couch, and he stared across the room with a sour expression. Glasses perched on his nose in dents that indicated he'd been wearing them for many years.

Seated next to him, his wife was busy on her phone. Her unnaturally-bright red hair spoke of frequent trips to the hair salon. She glanced up as I entered. Her eyes were highlighted by thick blue shadow and ringed with extra-long fake lashes.

"Good morning, everyone! You ready to go?" I said with a smile, trying to inconspicuously fan out my sweater. "Three Maidens' Manor is going to be a lot of fun!"

Mrs. St. Claire gave me a cheery hello, while her husband's

bored face changed into a wry grin. I turned to see what he'd been staring at.

Eliza Sue was at the drawing table, trying to open a small paper bag. Strewn across the table were her jacket, one of those fancy metal water bottles with a screw top, and a jaunty red sun hat. The bag was wrinkled, and I could only imagine how long she'd been trying to pack it with her belongings.

"Oh, hello, Georgie," she called to me. She flipped the bag to open it again.

"What's going on over here?" I asked, walking to the table.

Her brown curls quivered as she tried to jam the thin coat into the bag, but the bag kept collapsing due to the jacket's size. My hands twisted together behind my back, wanting to help her.

"It's just that this"—she blew away a fat curl that had fallen across her face—"this bag won't stay open." Frustrated, she gave the bag a few more flicks. The rustling papery sound of it was giving me anxiety.

I glanced over my shoulder at the waiting guests. Mr. St. Claire took off his glasses to clean them, and maybe to hide an eye roll. His wife nudged his shoulder and whispered to him to stop.

Their little interaction made me smile. People watching was

one of my favorite things about this job. I'd been running this tour for just under a year, after being offered the job by Aunt Cecelia. I called her Aunt Cecelia because she and my grandma had been best friends. My parents had died in a car accident when I was four. I barely remembered them, a fact that hurt more than I thought any actual memories would. It had been my grandma who had raised me, a quick-witted, loving woman who always had a hug. She'd spent so much time with Cecelia, that Cecelia had been just as likely to make cookies with me or threaten to tan my hide if I was late getting home as my grandma.

And, at the age of thirty, I guess you could say Cecelia rescued me. Just over a year ago, I was working nearly sixty hours a week in Pittsburgh as a paralegal to a lawyer who specialized in estates. A lot of the families in that area had Revolutionary war memorabilia that had been passed down through the generations, and part of my job was helping people figure out the value of those old heirlooms. It was fun, but exhausting. I'd been engaged to a man who always made me laugh and made me feel loved. You know what I mean by loved? That kind of feeling you get when you're scared to do something, but then you think of that special person and it makes you brave enough to do it anyway.

Derek. I smiled as I thought of him, now. He had some quirks that had driven me crazy. He'd liked to whistle all the time, but only three or four notes. He'd adored sneaking up behind me to scare me. He'd stubbornly insisted that tacos were better in a soft shell than a hard one, and he snored like crazy. But he'd loved me.

And I loved him.

Then one day changed everything. And when it did, Grandma was gone. So it had been Cecelia who reached out to help me try to pick up the pieces.

I sighed and pushed the thoughts about Derek from my head.

The front door slammed behind me and the Greens and Mr. Peterson rejoined us.

One more person, Sarah, a dark-haired athletic girl who'd proudly announced to us that she'd just won Iowa's Regional Amateur Women's Physique Championship, came in from the kitchen. The six guests stared at me, and then at Eliza Sue, as if trying to telegraph with the usual shuffling noises and coughs that they wanted me to make her hurry.

By now, Eliza Sue had managed to get her large water bottle and hat in the bag, but was still struggling with the coat. Her forehead wrinkled and her lips pouted as she tried to stuff the garment inside.

It was annoying to see her almost come undone. "Can I help?" I asked, with my hand held out.

She looked at me for a moment then passed over the mess. As

quickly as I could, I rolled up the coat to make it more compact and slid it next to the metal water bottle. The two items stuck out of the bag, looking like baguettes.

"If you'd like," I said, "your hat can sit right on top." I placed the hat over the other items and handed the bag to her like a sack of groceries.

"Okay." I turned back to the group with a clap of my hands. "Is everyone ready?"

A chorus of agreements rose around me. With a wave to Cecelia, who'd poked her white head out from the kitchen to wish us good luck, I led the guests to the waiting van.

The sunlight was bright and the scent of fresh-cut grass hung in the air. I squinted at my watch as I opened the van's side sliding door. We weren't running too late. Everyone climbed in and found a spot on one of the green vinyl seats.

I waited until they were all settled. Then, with a cheery smile, I said, "Good morning again, everyone!"

They greeted me back, with the exception of Eliza Sue, who still fretted with her bag. Finally, she scrunched it into the empty space under her seat.

"You're all in luck," I continued. "As you can see, it's a beautiful day. The drive out to the manor will be especially gorgeous. First, we'll be visiting the Three Maidens' Manor, and I guarantee there's some history there that will make your blood run cold. Then, I have lunch planned at the Boar's Head Tavern, and finally, I'll be dropping you all off back here, where you can continue with your dinner plans. Sound good? Everyone ready to go?"

After hearing their agreements, I slid the van door shut and hurried around to the driver's side. Once in the seat, I adjusted the rearview mirror, only to discover Mr. Peterson smiling back at me. He gave me another wink. I quickly averted my eyes and started the engine.

Old Bella, as I lovingly—and sometimes not so lovingly— referred to the van, gave a few harsh coughs before finally turning over. Another quick glance in the mirror showed the vehicle spewing its customary blue plume of exhaust, and I knew she was ready to go.

I shifted into gear, and with a lurch and a squeal from someone in the back seat, we were off.

Little did I know what we were really heading into.

CHAPTER 2

The drive to the manor was as incredible as I'd promised. I hummed happily, autumn being my favorite time of year. Spring was pretty amazing, and summer was nice, but you'd be hard pressed to find more vibrant fall colors anywhere else in the US. I'd sure missed it living in the city. It was like someone's grandma had laid her crazy quilt over the mountains. And the air! You couldn't beat that country air.

I breathed in deeply now, with my arm resting on the van's open window. Like I said, the warm temperature had resurrected the old barbecue ghost, but the fresh air had nearly chased it away.

We rattled down the country road that led to Three Maidens' Manor, my driver's seat bouncing hard on its worn-out springs. I had the seat pulled up as close as I could to be able to reach the gas and brake pedal, short girl problems.

I drove up the driveway and parked in front of the three-hundred-year-old building. It was a historical site now, but had once been an original Gainesville settler's home. And the grisly history of the building went back just as far. I jumped out, with everyone else slowly following.

As I waited for Eliza Sue to gather her things and disembark, I caught Mr. Peterson giving the young Mrs. Green a quick once-over with a small smile. Mrs. Green noticed his smile and brushed her long, blonde hair off her shoulder. She lifted an eyebrow above her tortoiseshell sunglasses, and he held her gaze as if challenging her. Slowly, she looked away.

Interesting.

I glanced at the elderly Mr. Green to see if he'd perceived the flirty look, but he was busy talking on his cell phone instead.

By now, Eliza Sue stood next to us, puffing as though getting out of the van took an exorbitant amount of effort.

I saw the bag in her hands. "Eliza Sue, would you like to leave that on the bus?"

She shook her head adamantly and clutched it closer. "I like to keep my water with me."

"Okay, then. Are we all ready?" I asked.

Mr. Green continued to talk on his phone, but gave me a slight wave in acknowledgement. The rest of the group responded positively as well. I led the little band up the porch to the entrance of the building. They followed me like good little ducklings after their mother.

I began with a sweeping hand motion. "There are many rumors that claim this building is haunted, and that the ghosts hate visitors. In fact, the manor was only recently opened to the public. When I grew up around here, no one dared to enter."

"You were scared?" Mr. Peterson scoffed.

I nodded. "Very. Every slumber party I ever attended always ended with a ghost story about this place."

"What's it haunted by? Soldiers?" Mrs. St. Claire asked, her red hair glowing in the sun. She batted her long eyelashes.

I nodded again. "The legend says not just one soldier, but several. After the battle at Fort Mifflin, a group of soldiers were sent out on a scouting expedition. The scouts, led by Captain William Heyword, ran into a band of redcoats, and the captain was severely wounded. They were too far away to return to the fort, so his remaining two soldiers carried him here, to Three Maidens' Manor. At the time, it was known to provide revolutionists safety as well as medical help."

"Let me guess. There was no help," Mrs. St. Claire

14

whispered. She stared at the house with her lips pursed in apprehension.

Mr. St. Claire's glasses flashed in the sunlight as he stood quietly by his wife's side. He tucked his hands into his pockets and waited for the answer.

"You're right," I said. "There definitely was not. The three sisters who lived here were loyalists, or tories. Unfortunately for the soldiers, that reputation of safety was part of a trap laid by the women. During the night, the women murdered the soldiers, dragged their bodies out through the field, and flung them into the Delaware River. It's said that the ghosts of the murdered Captain William Heyward and his soldiers haunt this house."

Mr. Green chuckled. I got it. Some people didn't believe in hauntings.

"That's how the story goes," I said mildly, shrugging.

He held the phone away from his mouth. "I'm sure it is. Like you said, a fun story over a campfire." He turned to his young wife, his white hair gleaming in the sunlight. "So, what do you think, honey? Think we're about to meet Casper?"

Mrs. Green shivered and grasped her designer bag closer to her side. "You know how I feel when you joke about things like that." She eyed the front of the building—a red brick exterior with a very plain entrance. "I'm not so sure about this."

"Stop. You can't believe this nonsense." Her husband gave her a sharp look.

"I kind of agree with you, Rachel," Mrs. St. Claire said to Mrs. Green. The red-headed woman scrutinized the building again, then suddenly jumped, looking startled.

"What's the matter?" I asked.

"What... what was that?" She pointed to a lace-curtained window on the second floor.

I glanced up, but didn't see anything.

She gave me a weak smile when I caught her eye. My response back was probably similar, honestly confused if she'd been joking or if she'd really seen something weird.

All right, I thought. *Enough of this.*

"I want to point out this interesting landmark." I directed their attention to the side of the door. Several holes marred the bricks. They had been conspicuously painted white to stand out against the red background.

"These right here are actual bullet holes from a battle that took place in 1779. By then, the three sisters had married. Lord Cornwallis himself gave the sisters three beautiful candleholders as a wedding gift to thank them for their loyalty. One of the couples moved to the town, but the two remaining fought in that battle. Rumor has it that one of the sisters hid the family's jewels somewhere on the property."

"Are we going to find some diamonds, then?" Mr. Peterson asked, tongue in cheek. He grinned rakishly at me and rubbed the cleft in his chin.

"Let's go inside and find out," I answered. "The curator will give us the tour and answer any questions you have."

I led my little group through the front door, our footsteps thumping against the wooden floor. Inside smelled like Pine-sol and old books. The light was dim, coming only from a single, lead-paned window.

Walking down the hallway to meet us was a short woman—shorter than even my five-foot-two—dressed in Revolutionary War attire. She wore a white cap and a calico dress covered by an apron.

"Hello!" she said, her voice high and cheerful. "Welcome to Three Maidens' Manor. Come in!" She waved her hands, encouraging us to move closer. "Scoot away from the door. There you go. There's plenty of space."

The eight of us crowded in the small foyer until the door was able to shut. A sharp creak sounded under Mr. St. Claire's foot, and we all jumped and then broke out in laughter.

"So!" the woman said with a happy clap of her hands. "My name is Mrs. Stilton, and I'm the curator here at Three Maidens' Manor. The spot where you are standing right now is where two of the sisters, along with their husbands, were killed in battle in 1779. The revolutionaries had finally come to take their revenge." She beckoned with her little hand. "Come on. Follow me."

The short woman led us down the hall with a sway of her hips. She brought us into the kitchen.

"Right there is the original butter churn, table, and chairs." Mrs. Stilton pointed. "And on this shelf are pieces of broken crockery that have been discovered on the property."

Mrs. Green asked her husband to snap a selfie of her beside the butter churn. He shook his white head impatiently, still on his phone.

Mrs. St. Claire walked over to the laced curtains. "Are these two hundred years old?" She brushed her red hair back from her face for a closer look.

"No, but they are old," Mrs. Stilton answered. "We try to use what antiques from the period we can find. But the rest are substitutes to help replicate the look of the late 1700's. The curtains are special because lace was a big deal back then. Women would tat yards of it to eventually edge her future curtains, handkerchiefs, and underclothes. She stored them in her hope chest."

"My goodness," Mrs. St. Claire murmured. "I'm glad we have Target these days."

The group laughed.

Mrs. Stilton guided the tour up a staircase, leaving Mr. Green behind to visit the bathroom. The group walked into the first of six bedrooms. We studied handmade headboards, clothing that was preserved behind glass, quilts, old hair brushes, perfume bottles, and razors.

As we left one bedroom and headed into another, I noticed both Sarah and Mr. Peterson were missing.

Just then, Eliza Sue nudged my arm. "Hey, I'll be right back. I have to use the little girl's room."

I nodded. I was starting to think that trying to keep this group all together was about as easy as herding cats. We walked into another room, where we learned about a straw tick mattress, conveniently cut in half to display the ticking, along with the rope bed-frame that held the mattress. There were boots, a shoeshine kit, and more. I glanced around and noticed Mr. Green had rejoined us at some point. He made a point to show us that his feet were nearly twice the size of the boots on display. His face creased into wrinkles as he laughed.

Mrs. Stilton watched us patiently before rounding us up again. "All right, everyone. If you can just follow me. We have one more area to cover." She led us back down the stairs. "Hang tight to the banister, these steps can be slippery. Now, where we're going is, perhaps, the spookiest place in the whole manor. It's where the sisters actually killed the soldiers."

We clattered down the stairs to the main floor. Eliza Sue came out of the bathroom and joined us.

"Come on. It's just this way." Mrs. Stilton opened a door in the hallway. Cold air rushed out of it, along with the scent of dirt.

"This is the root cellar," the curator continued. "The three sisters kept the soldiers down here, reassuring the men that it was to keep them hidden. Now, be careful. There are ten steps, so count them. Follow me."

She started down the stairs toward the pitch black, and the guests followed after her. I reached for the banister, noting it felt grimy. I could barely make out a string hanging from the ceiling, as Mrs. Stilton reached for it. She gave it a yank, but nothing happened.

"Oh, I'm sorry. The bulb must have burned out. Be careful, folks. Remember, there are ten steps. Don't worry, there's a light at the bottom." I heard an echo as Mrs. Stilton entered the space below.

"The basement is where most of the sisters' covert activities took place," she continued. "In one of the rooms down here, they actually kept a stock of weapons and ammunition for the English army. All of it was pilfered away, of course, when the revolutionaries got here. But there was a bayonet blade found buried in the ground. Possibly from the battle of 1779."

By now, the eight of us had traveled down the stairs after her and stood waiting in a huddle at the bottom. The only light came from the open doorway above.

I could hardly see Mrs. Stilton moving ahead. She stopped at what seemed to be a small side table. We began to squash together behind her.

"Hang on, everyone. I found the lamp," she said. "Just give me a second to turn on the light." She fumbled for the switch. There was a click. And then...

Boom!

Everyone screamed.

CHAPTER 3

A brilliant flash ripped through the darkness. I flinched at the sound of glass exploding. Blinded and disoriented, I groped about, trying to locate the wall. Screams filled the air. Someone bumped hard into my side, and then my foot was stomped on. From somewhere nearby, a man grunted.

"Get off of me," Mrs. Green yelled. I looked in the direction of her voice, but couldn't shake the bright echo of light my eyes were still seeing.

My fingers finally touched a wall. I stumbled closer to it just as everyone began talking.

"Breaker blew!" Mr. Peterson said, his voice infused with an extra measure of confidence. Relieved laughter rose around me.

Slowly, my eyes readjusted from the explosion. The hall was still dark, and everyone looked like shadows moving about.

"My goodness!" Mrs. Stilton exclaimed. "Is everyone okay?"

"I'm fine. Are *you* okay?" I asked, worried that the blast had burned her hand.

"I'm fine," she said. "Who's got a light?"

Someone pulled out their cell and clicked on the flashlight. The beam had a blue tint, making all the faces staring back appear extra pale as it swept the room.

Mr. St. Claire squinted hard behind his glasses as the light passed over his face. He threw up his hand. "Be careful with that, would ya?"

Several more cell phones flashed on as everyone assured each other they were fine.

"Honey?" Mrs. Green's young voice called out. And then even louder, "Honey?"

I looked around for her husband. The older man seemed to be missing.

Suddenly, she screamed and dropped to her knees. A

flashlight beam followed her. It splashed over Mr. Green lying on the floor.

He wasn't moving.

"Michael?" Mr. Peterson asked. He stooped down over the man. The flashlight's beam bobbled erratically across Mr. Green's body as whoever held the phone trembled.

"Honey, wake up!" Mrs. Green called, patting his cheeks. Her blonde hair fell over her face.

Dear heavens, did he have a heart attack?

"Michael!" Mr. Peterson said more firmly. He shook the old man's shoulder harder.

Mr. Green's jacket fell open.

"Oh, my word...is that blood?" I heard Mrs. St. Claire whisper.

Everyone fell silent. Someone trained their phone's light on his chest.

A blossom of red spread across the front of the man's oxford shirt. The cell's light glinted off something metallic. Sticking from the center of his chest, like the fletching of an arrow, was a silver handle.

Several people screamed. Someone called for lights. Someone else shrieked for help. I propelled myself through the crowd and dropped to my knees by the prone man's side.

"Everyone give him air!" It might have been a stupid thing to say. Mr. Green didn't look like air would help him now. I tentatively held two fingers to the side of the man's throat, but there was no pulse.

Mayhem broke loose. Mrs. Stilton returned, carrying a kerosene lantern. Mrs. Green cried in high-pitched keens, and Eliza Sue swept the poor woman into her arms. Mr. St. Claire blinked through his glasses at the body, dumbfounded, while Mr. Peterson spoke with the 911 operator. He seemed the calmest out of all of us, but I noticed even he rubbed his forehead in shock as he gave the operator the house's address.

I glanced around for Sarah, but she seemed to be missing. I couldn't be bothered to find her though, because Mrs. Stilton was trying to straighten Mr. Green's legs.

"No, just leave him be," I cautioned her with my hand up.

"He's... he.... Is it murder?" Mrs. Stilton whispered.

My gaze cut to Mrs. Green, but she was still sobbing on Eliza Sue's shoulder. Quickly, I gave Mrs. Stilton a grim nod.

"This can't be happening. This can't be happening," Mr. Peterson muttered. He'd put his phone away and was pacing in the hall. He bumped into Sarah, who was standing in a pool of light from the room at the end of the hall. She must have gone in there and turned it on.

Sarah reached out to Mr. Peterson as if trying to comfort the pacing man. He ignored her and abruptly turned and came pacing back like a caged lion.

"Maybe we can move her into the other room," Mrs. Stilton said. From the glare of the cell flashlight, I could see her nod in the direction of Mrs. Green, still sobbing in Eliza Sue's arms. I nodded. If the curator thought she could move the pair, that would be the best thing.

Mrs. Stilton walked up to them. "Would you like to go sit on the couch?" she asked in a quiet voice.

Mrs. Green didn't answer, but with Eliza Sue's help, Mrs. Stilton slowly guided her down the hall to the room. Their path was abruptly stopped by Mr. Peterson, who was returning from the other end.

"Will you stop that?" Mr. St. Claire snapped at Mr. Peterson. "Quit moving around!"

"What's it to you?" Mr. Peterson asked, his voice high with stress, his face hidden in the shadows.

I quickly got between them. "All right. Everyone just calm down."

"Calm down?" Mr. Peterson spun around to face me. "Someone just died!"

"And it wasn't an accident," Mr. St. Claire growled out, his glasses reflecting the light from the room.

I exhaled sharply. It gave me the shivers to think how adamantly he'd stated that.

I glanced at poor Mr. Green. Now that the flashlights had been taken off of him, I could barely make out his shape on the floor. The light from the end of the hall glinted off his well-polished shoes.

"I'm going outside," Mr. St. Claire said.

"I-I think you need to stay here," I said.

"I'm going to be sick," he growled again. And then he was stumbling down the hall the other way. I heard his shoes slap on the steps, and then distantly, the front door bang open.

Mr. Peterson glanced at me and then paced back the way where Eliza Sue had taken Mrs. Green.

I stood alone, my heart pounding, trying to think of what to do. The police were on their way here. I needed to keep the scene clean, keep everyone calm. Should I stay with the body? I glanced at the warm light spilling from the room ahead, and then back at the body.

My skin crawled.

A memory hit then. Just a whisper. So unexpected it brought a metallic taste to my mouth.

Derek.

"You know," a low voice said in my ear.

I jumped and a scream ripped out of me.

"Oh, my goodness. I'm so sorry," Mrs. Stilton apologized. Her face looked like a macabre crying mask with one side heavily in the shadows.

"Are you okay?" Mr. Peterson's voice was frantic as his silhouette filled the entry to the hallway.

"I'm f-fine!" I said, my voice feeling as weak as water.

"Again, I'm so sorry. I truly didn't mean to startle you," Mrs. Stilton repeated. "I just needed to share something. I didn't want the others hearing me."

"What?" I asked. The adrenaline caused my hands to shake. I wrapped my arms around myself, now grateful for the warm sweater.

"The alarm went off last night," she hissed.

"What alarm?" I whispered back.

"The manor's alarm. Like someone had broken in."

My mouth dropped. "Are you serious? Did you let the police know?"

"They met me out here. I searched through the house with them, but there was no one here."

The air felt like it had dropped twenty degrees since we'd first arrived. I shivered some more.

"This house is said to be haunted, you know." The curator leaned closer. I moved away, not liking her that close to me. Not now, not after everything that had happened.

She continued solemnly. "It's not the first time the alarm has gone off in the middle of the night. And sometimes things have been moved around."

"Was anything moved last night?" I asked.

Mrs. Stilton held up the lantern and shook her head. The light cast dark shadows under her eyes. "No. Nothing was moved. Nothing stolen. I figured that Captain Heyward and the soldiers were just bored last night."

"Soldiers... you mean..."

"Yes. The ghosts."

At her last word, I caught movement along the wall. A scream rose in my throat, ending in a weird gurgle when I realized it was Sarah. The young athlete slowly flexed her arm as she stood at the end of the hall, watching us.

Just then, I heard a clatter down the stairs. Mr. St. Claire arrived, followed by two police officers.

"Leslie," the first officer—a heavy-set man with a deep voice— addressed Mrs. Stilton.

"Charles," she said back.

"The soldiers again?" he asked, shining his Maglite down at poor Mr. Green.

I was taken by the word "again." Was the officer saying there were frequently dead bodies in this house? What exactly was going on around here?

CHAPTER 4

The officer's partner squatted next to Mr. Green before I could get a good look at him. The cop took Mr. Green's vitals, and then reached for his shoulder mic and called a code in.

I recognized the voice. It was Frank Wagner, Cecelia's grandson.

A part of me was overjoyed to see someone I knew here. An ally or something. But another part felt the exact opposite.

Frank and I had gone to school together. I used to see him all the time at my grandma's house as well as Cecelia's. And he'd always been an annoying know-it-all. Growing up, I swear his face had been perpetually marked by a slew of freckles and a scowl.

Our reconnection since I'd been back had been limited to a few, what Cecelia termed "family dinners' at the B&B. And he'd been as obnoxious as ever. So seeing him now, knowing he was the one who'd probably be interviewing me, kind of made my guts twist.

Mr. St. Claire stood rocking on his heels next to us, his hand over his mouth.

"You feel better?" I asked him quietly.

He nodded, and pushed his glasses up his nose.

The officer who had been talking with Mrs. Stilton turned to me. "I'm Sheriff Parker." He took out a pad of paper and a pen, the pen glinting weirdly in the kerosene light. He pointed it toward the room at the end of the hall. "How about we move down there to answer some questions?"

Frank had his gloves on and was patting down Mr. Green. Bile rose in my throat at the sight, and I hurriedly turned away. Mr. St. Claire must have felt the same way as me, because his shoulder bumped mine as he rushed past.

Sheriff Parker followed us into the other room. It was my first time getting a good look at the space, long and narrow. Two old-fashioned porcelain table lamps—the type with flowers painted on the white body—barely threw out enough light to brighten the room.

Mrs. Green sat on a wooden bench with Mrs. St. Claire's arm around her. The young woman seemed calmer now, and was wiping under her eyes with a tissue.

"This is the..." My mind struggled for a word that wouldn't send Mrs. Green into hysterics again. "The wife," I said.

Sheriff Parker squatted next to her and rested his hand on her knee. He began to ask questions to gather details about Mr. Green. Mrs. Green's voice was low as she answered him.

Mr. St. Claire bobbled on his heels at the end of the bench. He stared down at his red-haired wife, as if trying to grab her attention. She briefly glanced up at him and shook her head ever so slightly, before looking away.

Mr. Peterson still continued to pace, now from one end of this room to the other.

One, two, three, four... I silently counted the tourists. Who was missing? I glanced around, my gaze finally settling on Eliza Sue. She was seated on the floor behind a small secretary desk. But where was Sarah? Funny, how that girl kept disappearing.

"You tried to turn on the lamp and then there was a big explosion?" I could hear Frank ask Mrs. Stilton. The two of them came down the hall and joined the rest of us. Frank was tall and had to duck his head to get under the unusually low doorway.

"Yes, that's correct." Her hat-covered head bobbed in agreement.

"Had you been down here earlier?"

"Just last night, with Sheriff Parker and another officer." Sheriff Parker looked up when he heard his name. The curator continued, touching her chin with a finger. "Remember, we used flashlights down here?"

Sheriff Parker nodded.

Frank looked over at Mr. Peterson about to pace the hall. "Come join us, will you?"

Just then, we heard something clattering down the stairs. A crew of EMTs appeared in the hallway. Their shadows cast by the oil lamp on the table stretched toward us.

Mrs. Green stood at the sound of their footsteps. She glanced down the hall and seemed to waver on her heels.

"Someone catch her!" I yelled.

Just in time, Mr. Peterson caught her under the arms. He pulled her close to his chest as her sobs started once again. Mrs. St. Claire and Eliza Sue joined them as well. I could hear them murmuring to comfort the crying woman, but I couldn't understand the words.

We all shifted uncomfortably at the display of her grief.

Sheriff Parker nodded toward Mrs. Stilton. "Can you tell me where everyone was in approximation to the victim?"

The curator pursed her lips and stared back at Sheriff Parker blankly. "I'm not really sure. I was leading the group. I do believe Mr. Green was the closest person behind me though."

"Can anyone else confirm that?" the Sheriff asked the rest of us.

Mr. St. Claire shrugged, and pushed his glasses up his nose again. "It was dark. I was just trying to keep hold of my wife. Honestly, the whole thing was a hazard. Someone could have fallen and broken their neck."

"Shhh." Mrs. St. Claire frowned at her husband. She tucked her red hair behind her ear.

"It's not normally like this!" Mrs. Stilton snapped back. "The overhead light usually turns on when I pull the string."

"That's right. We tried it last night and the light was out," Sheriff Parker said. "You didn't replace it?"

Mrs. Stilton blushed. "Honestly, with the alarm and rushing down here at two in the morning, I was a bit flustered and exhausted. After we searched the place, I completely forgot about it."

"Wait, you were here earlier with the police? What's going on?" Eliza Sue asked.

Mrs. Stilton wrung her hands. "The alarm went off this morning. Sheriff Parker met me down here and searched the manor for intruders. I had to show up to check to see if anything was missing. After a careful examination, I was able to verify that nothing was. We thought it was just a glitch in the security system."

Sheriff Parker continued to take notes. "It seems we need to look a little deeper. And this time, not at ghosts."

Mrs. Stilton nodded.

"I realize you're all in shock, but we're going to take official statements from each of you. Don't leave town without stopping in at the station and speaking personally to me," Sheriff Parker warned.

The next few minutes were rough as the stretcher came and Mr. Green was loaded on to it. None of us watched him be carried upstairs.

Mr. Peterson offered to accompany Mrs. Green to the hospital. She shook her head in refusal, saying she'd rather ride with her husband. I told her I'd meet her at the hospital once I finished dropping the rest of the group off at the bed and breakfast.

Finally, we were able to make our departure from the Three Maidens' Manor. Everything felt numb to me. On my way down the hallway, I tripped over a large, brass candelabra that was sitting on the floor by the entry table.

"You okay?" Mr. Peterson asked, catching my elbow and steadying me.

I nodded wearily, and walked out to the van. Never had the scent of barbecue and corn been more welcoming. As we settled into our seats, I swore I could hear everyone breathe a sigh of relief.

I dropped the tourists back at Cecelia's. She met us at the front door, looking confused at our early arrival. The guests filtered into the living room and sat like statues on the couches. I could tell everyone was still trying to process what had happened.

"What on earth is going on?" Cecelia asked. My stomach felt like a leaden ball as I beckoned her to follow me into the kitchen. She shut the door and turned her questioning eyes toward me.

I cleared my throat, and tried to break it to her gently. But there was nothing *gentle* about the news. "It's Mr. Green. He was murdered at the Three Maidens' Manor."

Her hand flew up to her mouth. "No," she whispered.

"Frank was there," I added. "I suspect he'll be by soon. I have to get to the hospital to support Mrs. Green."

"The hospital?" she asked. "Oh, that's right. The morgue is in the basement."

I gave her a hug. "You okay, Auntie?"

She nodded and looked about her kitchen. "I suspect they'll need some food. Maybe hot cocoa. Poor things are probably in shock." She grabbed my arm. "But you... are you okay?"

I knew what she meant, and Derek's face floated in my mind. I nodded, but tears prickled my eyes. I squeezed them shut and shook my head.

She sighed sympathetically and patted my arm. "Don't worry, sweetheart. It takes time."

I licked my lip, now dry and painful. "One day at a time."

She nodded and patted my arm again. Then she spun away to the counter, and returned with a cookie. "Here, take this. You're looking pale. Your blood sugar is probably low."

I smiled and accepted the cookie. Trust Cecelia to try and fix everything with a little home-cooked food. But, amazingly, it usually worked. "Okay. I'll be back later."

"Go take care of Mrs. Green. Don't worry about the rest of the guests." She put on a kettle of water. "I'll bring them cookies and cocoa right now. If there's a group that needs a little refortification, it's them."

After another hug, I left, peeking into the living room as I passed. Half the group had their eyes closed, and the other half were on their phones or softly talking. I knew they were in good hands.

Once at the hospital, it took me a bit of time to locate the widow. After asking around, I finally found her in the chapel. It was a cold room, with stiff chairs and gray walls. The front glowed with a few lit candles. Another woman was with her.

Mrs. Green glanced up as I arrived, her eyes rimmed in red.

"Thank you for coming," she said. She glanced at the person next to her. "And thank you for waiting with me."

"Of course," the woman said. She stood and reached a hand toward me. I shook it as she said, "I'm Charity with grief services here at the hospital. We've been able to get ahold of Rachel's parents, and they're making plans to come support her."

The hospital worker took me off guard at the mention of Mrs. Green's parents. I glanced at the widow again, and her young age registered a little deeper. The poor girl was only in her twenties. This had to be a lot for her.

"Okay. Thank you." I sat down next to Mrs. Green and reached for her arm. "How're you doing?"

She shook her head, and turned her face toward the ceiling as her eyes puddled up. When she looked back at me, her face was pinched with grief. "I'm doing horrible. But the truth is, we've been expecting something like this for a long time," she whispered.

Her words chilled me to the bone.

CHAPTER 5

I gasped at her statement, taken off guard. "What? You expected this?"

Mrs. Green nodded. "He's gotten death threats numerous times."

"Did you say something to the police?" I asked.

"Yes, they know." She sighed and stared at the candles. I could see the tiny reflection's of the flames in the pupils of her eyes. "It was a knife. They got him right here." She pointed between her ribs. "There was someone else down there with us."

The thought gave me the shivers. Someone else? Well, that thought was better than the explanation that had been creeping around in the back of my mind.

She continued, musingly, "I thought Michael's secretary was supposed to join us on this leg of the trip, but I guess she didn't show. Actually, I don't even know if the secretary is a she. He?" Her bottom lip trembled. "Oh, Michael."

I swallowed. Watching her grieve was tearing my heart apart. I felt so helpless. "I'm sorry, Mrs. Green."

She glanced at me, her face flushed and tear stained. "Oh, please. Call me Rachel. I've never been comfortable with being called Mrs. Green."

I nodded and patted her arm. She took a deep breath to compose herself. "We've only been married a year. There's really so much about him I didn't know. I can't even name a single person who worked with him."

"You never spoke with them on the phone?"

She shook her head. "Michael was mostly retired. He rarely went into the office. In fact, most of his office days were really out on some golf course. He didn't want to be disturbed, and I didn't think anything about it." She bit her lip. "So many things I'm never going to know."

I tried to gently change the subject. "How well did you know the other guests? Did you spend time with any of them?"

She nodded. "Yes, we hung out with all of the guests. Played cards at night. Went out to dinner twice with the St. Claires. Honestly, if it was any one of them, there were easier ways they could have done this. Heck, they could have just broken into our bedroom at night."

I nodded. That was true. This group had hung out together nearly twenty-four seven.

But the Three Maidens' hallway was so narrow. How could another person have snuck in without any of us noticing?

There was a tap at the chapel's entrance. We both turned to look. A nurse walked in, her face showing deep compassion. She held a clipboard.

"I just need a few more things filled out," she said, passing it over to Mrs. Green. I got up to leave to give the young woman some privacy as they spoke about where the body would go. As I passed through the door, I cringed at the word "autopsy."

Of course there would be an examination. But to hear that word bantered around about a man I'd just seen that morning was too much.

My head ached from all the stress.

I walked down the hallway to a fish tank I remembered seeing earlier. The lights in the tank reflected water ripples on the far wall. I touched the glass, feeling the coolness under my fingers. Plastic green fronds bobbled in the airstream. White angelfish with long streaming wings sedately swam by. A sucker fish worked its way along the glass, cleaning the surface with its open mouth. Buried in the sand was a small pirate ship and pirate treasure. Every so often the treasure chest opened up and released a new stream of bubbles.

One of the people in my group could be the murderer.

There it was, the thought I'd been trying to hide. It jetted into my mind like the spurt of air bubbles through the water before me. There was no denying it, no way around it. It seemed improbable that another person was hiding among us when we huddled behind the curator before the lamp's light bulb blew up.

Mrs. Stilton didn't count. After all, how could she have known who I was bringing today? And I was out. Mr. Green, for obvious reasons, was out. Which left six.

I mulled them over in my head.

Mrs. Green, the young grieving widow. Her shock seemed very authentic. I couldn't believe someone was *that* good of an actor.

Mrs. St. Claire. The red-head hadn't behaved any differently than anyone would expect at the scene of a violent crime.

Mr. Peterson. Young and single, he'd been pacing the entire time. Obviously, he'd been agitated. But more than normal?

I bit my bottom lip and shook my head.

Mr. St. Claire had been out of sorts, but again that was expected in light of a murder.

Eliza Sue had been very compassionate toward Mrs. Green.

That left the last on my list, Sarah. The young body builder had been quiet after the murder. I barely remembered seeing her at all.

I caught sight of the frown I was wearing in my reflection in the aquarium glass. Something about Sarah was bothering me. What was it? It was on the tip of my tongue—

"Oh, there you are!"

I jumped and spun around. Mrs. Green had unexpectedly popped up behind me.

"I'm sorry!" we both said simultaneously.

And then we laughed.

The laughter was odd, and I tried to rein it in. But then Mrs. Green snorted, which made me laugh harder. Maybe we just needed some stress relief, or maybe we were both crazy, but we laughed like two loons. She stumbled forward and clung to me for balance.

Finally, the giggles settled down into a few humming sighs. She wiped tears from under her eyes.

"I think I'm a lunatic," she confessed.

"If you're one, then I am one, too." I hugged her briefly. She snuffled a bit and then took a few deep breaths.

When she seemed to have settled down, I asked, "You ready to get back home?"

She hesitated, her eyes going wide.

I suddenly pictured how she would feel going back to her empty room at the bed and breakfast. Her husband's clothing strewn about from where he'd left them that morning, his toothbrush by the sink.

"Hey," I added, "I only have a couch at my apartment, but you're welcome to it, if you'd rather..."

She nodded right away. "Yes, that would be great. If you're sure that's okay? My parents will be here some time tomorrow."

"You got it," I said and guided her to the door. "Let's get out of here."

On the way home, I took a detour through the drive-through at a fast food restaurant. She asked for a burger, but as we pulled back onto the street, the paper bag sat unopened on her lap. She stared out the passenger window. Street lights strobed across her face as we passed under them. She didn't say a word the entire way home.

Parking was usually slim around my apartment complex. But tonight we were lucky, and there was an open spot in front of the brick building.

I pulled the van into it and climbed out. Rachel moved slowly, as though she were an eighty-year-old woman. With a sigh, she finally got out. I led the way to the building's huge front steps and front door.

The apartment building required a security code to open the doors. I quickly punched it in, and we walked inside.

The entryway was dimly lit with wall sconces. Rent was inexpensive, but the place was respectable and clean. I loved how it still held a lot of its old-world charm in the wood-hewn staircase and heavy, carved bannister. I walked up to the fourth floor with her trailing behind me.

My legs were used to the trek now, but I remembered how they burned when I'd first moved here. I wondered how she was doing.

The scent of spaghetti and onions greeted us as we rounded the landing to my floor. I knew it was coming from Mrs. Costello's place, two doors from my own. There were only four apartments per floor. Like I said, it was a clean place, and everyone was super friendly.

I brushed my short hair back from my face and unlocked my door. Once inside, I grimaced at how it was pitch-black inside. When would I ever remember to leave on a light? I clicked on the lamp, then turned to check on Rachel.

She stood in the entry and clung to her purse like it was a security blanket. Too late, I realized she'd left the food in the car.

"You want me to go get your burger?"

She glanced around my apartment like a stray dog afraid it was about to be kicked. Slowly, she shook her head and shut the door. I walked into the kitchen area and set about making her some chamomile tea. From the clock on the stove, I saw it was already past nine. She followed me and dragged out a chair from the table to sit, scraping its legs against the tile as if she were too feeble to lift it.

After a moment, she dug into her pocket and pulled out an object. Metal flashed in her fingers, like she had a coin. She rolled it around in her palm. I removed the mug from the microwave and took a minute fussing about for some sugar and a spoon. Then I carried everything over to the table and set it before her.

She stared at the steaming cup before her gaze moved up to

me. Her eyelashes were wet. Slowly, she opened her fingers to show what lay in her palm.

A wedding ring.

"They gave this to me before they took him away," she said simply.

I could feel my eyes start to sting. She slipped the ring on her finger, where it hung, overly large, before trying it on her thumb. With a sigh, she dipped the tea bag in and out of the mug and added some sugar.

I didn't know what to say. It was perhaps cowardly of me when I turned away to search the cupboards for some cookies. I almost gave up finding any, until I spotted some weird gingersnaps that were probably hard as rocks. Cecelia had brought them the last time she came for a visit. She liked to dip them in her tea.

Well, we do have tea, I thought, and brought the box back to the table.

"Thanks," she said, sounding numb. I snagged a napkin from the Lazy Susan, and shook a few cookies onto it. She scooped one up with trembling fingers and took a bite. Immediately, her eyes flew open at the loud crunch.

"Aunt Cecelia dips them," I said, indicating her tea.

She nodded and, with a weak grin, dunked the remainder.

"Dipping's good." She bit into the cookie. Her shoulders relaxed. "This is the first thing I've eaten all day."

I nodded, thinking about how I hadn't seen her eat much of anything since she'd checked in to the B&B. I chalked it up to her trying to keep a slim figure.

The silence grew between us. It was obvious we were talked out.

After another ten minutes or so, I gave her a quick tour to show her where the bathroom was, and hauled out a couple pillows and blankets from the closet for the couch.

"You want the TV on?" I asked, remote in hand.

She sank to the sofa and felt the edge of the pillowcase. With a sigh of weariness, she moved the pillow to the end of the sofa and laid her head down. "I'm fine," she answered.

I shook out one of the blankets and placed it over her. "Okay. I'll just be in the other room. You need anything, you come get me."

She nodded and turned on her side.

I went into the kitchen for my sleeping pill. Ever since Derek had died, I'd been plagued by nightmares and couldn't sleep. I had to have a little help. Soon maybe, I'd try to brave the night without it. But tonight was not that night.

When I passed back through the living room again, she was completely still with her eyes closed. But I knew she wasn't sleeping. She wanted to be alone. I got that. And when I shut my bedroom door, I heard her start to cry.

I knew what that was like, too. And my heart squeezed for her. I went to my bed and hugged my pillow, feeling helpless once again.

CHAPTER 6

$\mathcal{T}$he smell of fresh-brewed coffee filled my dreams. I woke up with a start at the sound of a cupboard shutting. My hand bumped the pepper spray container under my pillow as I rolled over. *Oh, yeah! Rachel's here.* I shrugged into my robe and stumbled from my room and into the kitchen.

Rachel was sitting at the table. She smiled, but her eyes were puffy.

"Hey, lady," I said. I glanced around to see the kitchen was clean and coffee had already been made.

"Hi, yourself." She lifted her mug. "I hope you don't mind that I made myself at home."

"No, of course not." I got another mug and filled it with coffee. The rich scent cleared my head. I pulled out a chair and immediately laughed.

Rachel was dunking stale gingersnaps into her coffee.

"I can do better than that. Want me to make you some eggs?"

She shook her head. "No, thanks. She glanced down at her phone. "By the way, I asked Eliza Sue to bring me some clean clothes. She's here, now, and wants to know what the code is."

"2262," I told her, and then hurried to my room.

In the master bathroom, I wrinkled my nose at my reflection in the mirror. I loved the change I'd made to short hair. But I was finding it took longer to get it to look nice. Before, with my long hair, I could always swoop it up into a bun. But with short hair, I actually had to *do* something with it. I wet my brush and smoothed it out—dirty blonde like my mom used to have. It was one of the memories I still had of her. Sunlight on her head as she handed me my Easter basket and told me we were going to look for eggs. I glanced at my hand now, still remembering how it had slipped into her hand. Blonde hair and soft hand squeezes.

"Miss you, mom," I whispered, turning back toward my room to dress.

A long flannel shirt and yesterday's jeans completed my outfit. After slipping on sneakers, I returned to the kitchen.

Eliza Sue was standing in the room alone, looking awkward. I guess Rachel had left her to get ready because the young widow was nowhere in sight.

"Oh, I'm sorry," I said. "I just wanted to be dressed when you showed up."

"No worries." She glanced around, her brassy curls immune to the movement of her head. "Nice place you have here."

"Thank you. Do you want some coffee?" By now, I'd walked over to the couch that was still strewn with blankets and pillows. Rachel must have changed her mind at some point during the night about the TV, because it was on, with some game host yelling out the dollar amounts of prizes.

"No, that's okay," Eliza Sue answered. "That's some hike up those stairs, though. Whew!"

I nodded as I tossed the pillow up on a shelf. "It really is, but I love it here."

Rachel came out of the bathroom as I started to fold one of the blankets.

"Oh! Let me take care of this mess," the blonde woman said, reaching for the blanket.

"Don't worry about it." I waved my hand at her. "I'll probably be curled up in it tonight."

Rachel had yesterday's clothing stuffed into the bag that Eliza Sue had brought. She looked around uncertainly, before dropping it to the floor. Her hands covered her eyes as she groaned.

"I just can't believe this is happening."

Eliza Sue patted her arm and made a few sympathetic sounds, her eyes flickering a worried look at me.

There was nothing any of us could say, no matter how badly we wanted to fix this, that would bring any measure of relief. I joined them, and we stood there, holding Rachel up as grief tore through her body like waves against a reef.

I swore I was going to find the person who had caused this.

Finally, her tears abated. She dabbed at her eyes and sighed deeply. It was easy to see she was worn out.

A chime came from Rachel's bag. She wearily stooped over and dug through it, eventually coming out with her phone. She read the text. "My parents are there, now."

"Come on, dear. Let's get you back to them," Eliza Sue picked up the bag and began to guide her to the door.

I grabbed my purse, and we headed out, with me locking the door behind us.

Going down four floors brought the expected comments. "I can't believe there's no elevator," Eliza Sue grumbled.

"You get used to it, I swear," I answered, opening the front door. I left the two of them on the stoop as Rachel was giving Eliza Sue a hug and thanking her.

I started Old Bella and was surprised to see the passenger door open.

"You coming with me?" I asked.

Rachel shrugged and climbed in. "You don't mind, do you?"

"No, of course not."

"Eliza Sue was sweet, but I just don't want to talk right now."

I nodded, getting that. We'd kind of established silence was okay between us last night. She buckled her seatbelt, and I shifted the van into gear. We headed to the Baker Street Bed and Breakfast, with Eliza Sue following us in her car.

My aspirations to quickly get to the B&B were halted when an Amish buggy, complete with its orange triangle fastened to the rear, pulled out directly in front of us.

I smiled sheepishly at Rachel. "It's going to be a while. You might want to text your parents and let them know."

She searched for her phone. As she typed, I noticed her husband's ring was still around her thumb.

Twenty minutes later, we finally arrived at the bed and breakfast. A black Lincoln was parked in the driveway.

As we walked to the veranda, the door opened, and a woman about ten years older than me stepped out. Her husband, an older man with winged gray hair, wearing a blue sweater vest, was behind her.

"Mommy!" Rachel cried and sprang the rest of the way up the stairs. The three of them hugged.

Eliza Sue entered the B&B first, with me following behind. As quietly as possible, I shut the door.

The scent of cinnamon and bacon was nearly tangible, hitting me like a soft feather pillow. Wanting to check in first with Cecelia, I scurried past the entrance of the dining room, where the group of guests sat around the table.

Clanging metal rang out as I walked into the kitchen. Cecelia was bustling about the stove, flipping eggs in a huge skillet. Her white hair was piled high in a bun, her cheeks pink from the heat.

"Hi, Auntie," I said.

She jumped. "Young lady! You have to quit scaring me! Drag your feet or something." And then softer, she continued,

"How are things? How is Mrs. Green? I assumed she found her parents?"

I smiled at being called a young lady, now that I was thirty-one. "Yeah, she's out there with them right now."

She pursed her lips and looked thoughtful. "That poor thing. Would you like some coffee?"

I walked over to the coffee pot and waiting mugs, and helped myself. "How were things yesterday?"

"Oh, my goodness. It was a late night around here. The sheriff came back around eleven and took statements from everyone who was still awake." Slap. An omelet hit the plate. She poured another ladleful of eggs into the empty pan. "Except for that one gal. Sarah."

Odd. I could feel my forehead knotting. "Oh, really?" I took a sip of coffee.

"Yep. She spent the entire evening in her room. Haven't seen her this morning either, come to think of it."

Her mention of Sarah reminded me of that nagging feeling I'd had yesterday. Never did figure out what it meant.

Slap! More eggs hit a plate. "Can I get you something, hun?" Cecelia's dress swished as she spun around, her legs clad in tan support hose.

"No, thanks. I'm good."

Carefully, she layered the plates on her arm.

"Here. Let me carry a few." I picked up the remaining plates and followed her out to the dining room. Everyone called out good morning as I entered.

Cecelia placed the plates around the table, with me following as she unloaded mine. "Your waffles will be right up," she reassured Mrs. St. Claire. The woman was in the process of clipping her red hair back at the base of her neck as she said thank you. She didn't have on makeup, and her eyes looked strangely bare without the blue shadow and long black fake lashes.

I walked back to the kitchen and brought out the waffles. Cecelia returned with the coffee decanter. She pulled a container of real maple syrup from her apron pocket and set it before Mrs. St. Claire. "Can I get you guys anything else?" she asked, as she walked around refilling the coffee mugs.

I retrieved my coffee cup from the kitchen and then sat at the end of the table. The guests had already dug into the food, and fruit plates, glasses half filled with orange juice, and muffin wrappers littered the tabletop.

"Is Rachel here?" Mrs. St. Claire leaned over to whisper to me.

I nodded, still taken aback by how different she looked without makeup. "She's outside with her parents."

"Poor lady. Everyone's just falling apart. Last night was so strange." She shook her head and then cut a corner of her waffle. "Which reminds me, has anyone seen Eliza Sue or Sarah today?" she asked a bit louder.

Nearly everyone shook their head. Mr. Peterson was the only one who didn't respond. He sat with a confused expression on his handsome face.

"Well, I saw Eliza Sue this morning," I answered. "Mrs. Green texted her to bring by some stuff."

Mr. Peterson reached for the salt shaker.

It tipped over and Mrs. St. Claire gasped. "Quick! Throw the salt over your shoulder. It's bad luck!"

I looked at her, a little surprised at how adamant she was.

"I mean it! Please!" Her eyes widened with desperation and fear.

Carefully, Mr. Peterson swept the salt into his hand and threw it over his shoulder. As soon as he did, she settled back in her chair and, as if realizing how she sounded, her cheeks turned pink. She glanced bashfully at the rest of us at the table.

"I'm sorry," she said. "But I think we've all had more than our fair share of bad luck, don't you agree? I didn't want to test it any more."

Her husband pushed up his glasses and patted her hand. "It's okay, dear. Who could blame you?" he said under his breath.

Mr. Peterson cleared his throat and leaned toward me. He looked so serious that I leaned in his direction, too. His voice was low as he asked me, "You know how Mrs. St. Claire asked if any one of us saw Eliza Sue?"

I nodded, not sure where this was going.

"Well, I did, actually. Last night. Or, early this morning, I mean. And it's not the first time that's happened."

The small talk around the table stopped as everyone tried to listen in.

His gaze flicked around the table and his jaw tightened. He obviously didn't like being the center of attention. Sitting up, he stabbed at his eggs and took a bite.

"What?" he asked, staring around at everyone. "It was two. I needed to get some fresh air. I was just going to tell Georgie that Eliza Sue was outside, too."

"Really?" I said, slightly surprised. "What was she doing out there?"

"I can tell you what I was doing."

Everyone's head turned to look at the person who spoke from behind me.

Eliza Sue.

CHAPTER 7

*E*liza Sue sauntered into the dining room with a cool expression on her face. Her dark helmet of curls were as stiff as ever.

"Good morning again," I said to her. Her gaze moved toward me and her lips tightened. With a small smile, she pulled out a chair next to Mr. St. Claire, who shifted uncomfortably closer to his wife.

"Good morning, everyone. Seems I'm the topic of conversation this morning, hmm?"

Cecelia bustled in with a cup of coffee. She set it before Eliza Sue. "What can I get you for breakfast? We have a fruit platter, cereal, eggs to order, and waffles."

"A plate of fruit would be delightful," she replied.

Cecelia nodded and disappeared back into the kitchen.

"So, what were you doing outside that late?" Mrs. St. Claire asked. "I know it was a crazy night. Just processing your thoughts?"

Eliza Sue glanced down at her mug of coffee. She cupped it as though to warm her fingers. "I often go for a walk before bed. It clears my head, and the moon's been beautiful, lately. Besides, after everything that had happened, I couldn't sleep."

That spurred the rest of the group into talking.

"Oh, me either!" Mrs. St. Claire exclaimed.

Her husband nodded and adjusted his glasses. "It's true. You tossed and turned all night. Stole the covers like you were making a beehive."

"Well, you snored," she shot back sweetly.

Mr. Peterson sighed. "I couldn't quit thinking about poor Rachel." That statement shut the conversation down again as a few anxious faces glanced in the direction of the door as if expecting her to appear.

Cecelia came into the dining room once again. She set down a plate of fruit in front of Eliza Sue and then quietly cleared some of the plates.

"Here, you can take mine," Mrs. St. Claire said, pushing it forward. She'd scarcely eaten.

"You sure, honey? You want me to make you something else?" Cecelia asked.

Mrs. St. Claire set the napkin next to the plate. "No, I'm finished for now." She shrugged thin shoulders. "I'm just so upset about everything."

"Glad to see everyone's here," came a deep voice from the dining room doorway.

Inwardly, I groaned. I knew who that voice belonged to.

Frank.

Last night, we didn't really get a chance to talk. Maybe I was crabby this morning because of lack of sleep, but his tone brought me right back to the time he yanked my braid because I was winning at the game Stratego.

I turned toward him. Yep, there he was. All six-foot plus of him, dressed in full police gear. He frowned as he studied us. We stared back at him like he was a coyote who'd invaded the chicken coop.

And we were the chickens.

"Grandma," he said to Cecelia. "Can I have a minute to talk to your guests?"

She nodded and left the room.

Mr. St. Claire cleared his throat. "Officer...?"

Frank's gaze snapped toward him. "Officer Wagner. I stopped by to let you know that you'll be getting calls to come to the station today to make an official statement. And it's by the authority of Sheriff Parker that no one make any plans to leave Gainesville for a few days."

Mr. St. Claire let out a scoffing laugh. "You can't be serious. I can't leave town?"

Frank stared at him, his thick eyebrows lowering. "Does it look like I'm joking? You have a problem with that?"

"Yeah, actually. I do have a problem. I have businesses to take care of, things to do."

Frank looked over at me, and I winced. I could feel it coming. He was about to put me on the spot. "Georgie, when's this tour supposed to be over?"

"Err." I didn't dare look at the St. Claires. "Technically, we just had today and tomorrow planned, with people free to leave after that."

Frank shifted his gaze back toward Mr. St. Claire. His eyes were piercing and blue. "So, it seems like two more days were already in your schedule. Now why exactly do you need to leave before then?"

"Yeah, we *planned* to stay. Until one of our own was murdered, which kind of ruined the idea of having fun. You can't really blame us for wanting to cut our vacation short."

"Blame, Mr. St. Claire? Odd word for you to use."

"I don't see what's so odd about it. You're asking us to justify why we want to go home."

Frank's jaw tightened. "No, I'm telling you why you're not free to go home. You are all under investigation."

"Surely, you can't be serious!" Mr. St. Claire roared, while his wife's mouth dropped open. Around me, more gasps could be heard. I didn't see what was so surprising about that revelation. As far as we knew, we were the only ones there. Of course we were being investigated.

I swallowed hard. That included me, too.

"I want my lawyer!" Mr. St. Claire threw down his napkin.

"You're free to call your lawyer. Right now, we just need a statement. You have a problem for some reason giving a statement, sir?" Frank straightened, his shirt tightening across his broad chest. "Because that will definitely change how we decide to handle this."

Mr. St. Claire settled back in his chair. He patted his wife's hand. "I'll call him later. Don't worry."

Frank eyed him for a moment more before addressing the rest of the group. "Like I said, we have your phone numbers. This is a normal part of the investigation, and we appreciate your cooperation. Please respond to the requests for a formal interview in a timely manner. Our goal is to get through this quickly and get you all back on your way. Just don't leave town without getting it cleared."

He put his hat back on his head and, after a quick goodbye to Cecelia in the kitchen, headed back out the door.

Frank left all of us sitting there in different degrees of shock, looking like it really had been a case of a coyote in the hen house, after all.

CHAPTER 8

s soon as Frank closed the front door, the room erupted into chaos. Mr. St. Claire yelled about the incompetence of the Gainesville police while dialing his phone.

Mr. Peterson shouted randomly, "Calm down! Everyone, calm down!"

Eliza Sue pulled at my shirtsleeve. "What do we do now? I'm scared!"

In the midst of this, Sarah sauntered in. The young athlete took one look at all of us in the dining room and spun straight around to go back.

"Wait!" Mr. St. Claire yelled, after spotting her. "Where've you been? You're in the thick of this, too!"

She turned toward us as if resigned, twisting her brown hair up into a sloppy bun. "In the thick of what? I have no idea what's going on. I just want to get some breakfast."

Cecelia rescued her. "What can I get for you? I can make you some eggs."

"Coffee to start. And maybe some bacon?" the young woman asked.

Cecelia nodded and disappeared back into the kitchen.

"Where *were* you last night?" Mr. St. Claire asked again. His eyes glared behind his glasses. I took note of his aggressive tone.

"I was doing this weird thing called sleeping," Sarah snapped back as she sat down at the table. "It's what normal humans do. Not that you would know anything about that."

My eyebrows rose. What was going on between those two? I wished I'd taken the opportunity to get to know Sarah better. I knew she competed in fitness competitions. She'd mentioned once that she ran kickboxing classes at her gym. She was unusual, because not many young women take vacations by themselves. Somewhere in her twenties, she was closer to Rachel's age than anyone else in the group. With the St. Claires and Eliza Sue in their early forties, Mr. Peterson was the next closest in his thirties. There really was no one in the group she had anything in common with. I could understand why she went to bed early last night.

Cecelia came in, bearing a mug of coffee and a plate of bacon. She set them before Sarah and then whisked out a napkin from her apron pocket. "Anything else, dear?"

"No, thank you," Sarah said, glancing up at her with a small smile.

"Well, you just missed Officer Dudley Do-Right ordering us to stay here," Mr. St. Claire snapped.

I struggled not to sigh. That man was just acting unpleasant. Instead of reacting, I left the table, not wanting to rehash the entire explanation one more time.

"I'll see you guys later," I told the group.

Some fresh air was what I needed, but since Mrs. Green and her parents were still occupying the front porch, I headed for the back door.

It was another beautiful day. Sunlight streamed through the bare branches of the maple trees, but the air held a crisp note that predicted it would be a cooler day. I walked down the steps and into the leaf-strewn back yard. The grass felt wet and marshy under my feet.

Ahh. Peace and....

"Georgie!" Mr. Peterson yelled, slamming the back door.

I flinched. I just needed five minutes. Just five minutes alone. Carefully, I arranged my face into a welcoming look, and then spun toward him.

"Mr. Peterson. You tracked me down."

"Yeah, well." His good-looking face appeared gaunt this morning. He fished a cigarette from his front pocket and lit it with the expertise of a long-time smoker. Quickly, he exhaled a plume of white smoke. "We never did finish the conversation I started earlier."

"Oh, yes. That's right." I remembered.

I glanced up at him as we slowly walked along the length of the house. He was quite a bit taller than my five-foot-two.

"I'm going to tell you something, just between you and me." He squinted and pointed his fingers holding the cigarette at me. "Can you keep a secret?"

I thought about that for a second. What kind of secret was it? "Of course."

He took another drag. "I don't trust that St. Claire fellow. He's got something he's hiding."

We paused under an old apple tree. "Oh, yeah? What makes you say that?"

Mr. Peterson checked behind him. As if reassured that no one was coming, he quickly whispered to me, "I overheard something last night. When I was outside."

"What did you hear?"

"It was when I was walking around the house. It was a hot night, and the St. Claires had their window open. She was telling him they needed to be careful. Very careful."

The hair at the base of my neck prickled at the tone of his voice. "And?"

"He told her to shut up. That they were safe. She just needed to keep her trap shut." His dark eyes stared into mine. "I tried to hear more, but that's when I saw Eliza Sue come around the corner. I had to hurry over to her so she didn't yell a greeting and give me away."

"Wow, the worst timing ever." I kicked a pinecone, my hair falling into my face.

Air hissed from between his gritted teeth in frustration. I looked at him in surprise.

"You have no idea. Besides, I swear I know him from when I worked in Brooklyn. If he is who I think he is.... " Mr. Peterson flicked the ash off the end of his cigarette, then tossed it over the hedge that separated the bed and breakfast from the neighbor's house.

I was about to respond when I heard an explosion of anger from the other side of the hedge.

"Get your confounded cigarette trash away from my yard. You're nothing but a tar chimney!" a grouchy old man's voice yelled. The cigarette butt sailed back over the bush.

I stared at it for a second before glancing around for the speaker.

Mr. Peterson laughed. "You got it, old man." He pushed the toe of his shoe into the butt, smashing it into the wet grass.

Said old man popped up, scowling, over the hedge. He held clippers in his hand. "This old man can still take on the likes of you. You're about as useless as a chocolate teapot. Get out of here." He shook the clippers in his hand.

"I'm sorry about that!" I reached for Mr. Peterson's elbow and tried to move us away from the hedge. And then quieter, "Come on, let's go back inside."

The man gave us another fierce glare. Mr. Peterson shot him a wink.

"Come on, I said." I tugged him harder by his arm. Reluctantly, he let me lead him to the back door. "Go inside and take a breather. Maybe get another muffin or something." I opened the door for him.

His eyes caught mine, and the humor drained away. "You'll keep all of that a secret?"

I nodded. "Don't worry. I won't say a peep."

He nodded and walked inside. As the door shut behind him, I breathed a sigh of relief.

I wearily sat on the top porch step and stared out into the back yard. I had to find a hobby. I needed a real way to relax.

The wind was growing sharper. I pulled my hoody a little tighter around me. That still didn't cut it, so I stood to zip it. At my foot was another white cigarette butt, this one squashed and bent in half. A quick glance showed there were several others hidden under the edge of the porch.

I walked the length of the bed and breakfast, opposite the way Mr. Peterson and I had just been. A maple tree marked the east corner, where the St. Claires' room was. Cherry-patterned chintz curtains were pulled back from the window, and I could just catch a glimpse of a quilt-covered four-poster bed. I looked away so as not to appear peeping.

It was then that I saw it. Stamped out at the base of the tree was another cigarette butt.

Mr. Peterson *had* been here. Was this proof of what he'd overheard?

Puzzling over it, I walked out into the back yard. Cecelia's flower garden badly needed to be pruned. Black rose heads still clung to some of the bushes, while other flower stalks lay in wilted piles.

I turned around and studied the back of the bed and breakfast.

Nearly all of the windows had their curtains pulled back to allow the daylight in. All except one. The window above the St. Claires'.

I frowned as I studied it. The window was nearly hidden by a large branch of the maple tree. But I still saw something that made me take note.

There was no screen covering the window.

A quick scan over the rest of the house proved all the other screens were firmly in place on the other windows.

Weird. I'd need to ask Cecelia about that.

Turning, I went deeper into the yard, taking care not to let my feet get tangled in the wet, overgrown grass. Marking the back property line was a stone fence. It stood about four feet high, and had been stacked there who knows how many years ago. Maybe even by the original owners.

I loved this area, so rich in history. History was one of my favorite parts about being a paralegal for the estate lawyer.

There were many antiques the clients knew nothing about. It'd been so satisfying to do the research and figure it out.

But after Derek, I just couldn't continue. There were too many unanswered questions as to what had happened to him. I had to get away.

I reached out to touch the bark of an apple tree growing next to the stone fence. Centuries ago, this home had an apple orchard. But now most of the trees were gone, leaving slowly rotting stumps.

I held on to its trunk as I gazed past the rock wall. There wasn't a lot to see, just an over-grown field, most likely once cultivated by a farmer. Now it was a sea of waving grass. I could just make out an old farmhouse and a smudge of trees in the distance.

I glanced up into the gnarled limbs of the apple tree. The branches had grown haphazardly, intertwining in their search for the sun. There was a smooth spot marking one of the intersections, and I could picture someone using it as a seat. I wondered how many kids had climbed into its branches and daydreamed while eating an apple.

Try it. Do it. I smiled at my goofy inner voice. Well, why not? I reached for a branch above my head and started to climb.

Well, I did not swoop up into the tree like I had envisioned. Instead, my feet kicked helplessly as I searched for purchase along the smooth trunk. Visions of a fat hobbit trying to get over a fence filled my mind, and I let go, feeling foolish.

Maybe a visit to the gym wouldn't be out of line.

It was then that I saw it. Something small. Something hidden in the weeds in the crook at the base of the tree.

Another cigarette butt.

But this one had red lipstick marks on the end.

CHAPTER 9

ho wears red lipstick? I rifled through my memories of the houseguests, trying to think. The only one who came to mind was Mrs. St. Claire. But she didn't smoke.

The cigarette butt was new. It didn't show signs of being exposed to the elements very long. But that didn't conclusively mean it came from someone at the house. After all, Mr. Peterson had thrown one into the neighbor's yard. Someone else could have very well done that here.

A gust of wind tore through the field and rattled the branches above me. It was too cold to be out any longer in just a hoody. I turned and hurried back into the house.

Inside, the kitchen was warm and cozy. Cecelia was there, her mixing bowl on the counter. It made me happy to see it, remembering it from childhood. Made from stoneware, it had a blue flower on the front and blue stripes along the top.

Cecelia had on her glasses and was sprinkling the counter with flour. She pulled her rolling pin from the drawer— another staple from my childhood. It was a deep honey brown with red handles.

"How you doing, GiGi? Cold outside?" she asked.

"Freezing." I smiled at her use of my childhood nickname and rubbed my arms. "By the way, I think we made your neighbor mad."

She upturned the bowl onto the floured surface and began to work the dough. Her strong wrists flicked until the dough was punched down and somewhat round. She dusted her pin and began to roll.

"Uh oh," she said, frowning slightly. "Not Oscar."

"Oscar?" I asked.

"Mr. O'Neil. He's new to the area."

"How new?" Around these parts, new had its own meaning.

"Oh, about nine or ten years. He and his wife moved here after he retired. Poor man. Lost his wife last year."

I cleared my throat. Her words hit that spot I hadn't been prepared to protect.

Cecelia didn't say anything more. Her pin made soothing sounds as she rolled. I sat at the table and watched, fascinated. I'd always been this way, nearly hypnotized by pie making. The precise strokes that turned the lump of dough into a shape. The neat way she flipped it over the pin and laid it in one swoop into the pie pan. Then came the filling—today a bowl of cherries coated in sugar and spice that would turn into a red syrup that blended perfectly with a spoonful of homemade vanilla bean ice cream.

She poured the filling in and gently nudged the cherries around to fill the pan. Next came a bit more flour to dust the counter and then the rest of the dough. In moments, Cecelia had the dough rolled out and was cutting it into strips.

"You know, I have a little something that I wasn't sure if I should share."

My ears perked up. "Really? I can already tell I want to hear this."

She glanced at me. "It's about Mr. Green."

My stomach dropped. "Okay...."

Cecelia smiled faintly. "Once upon a time, I knew him. It feels like a lifetime ago." She chuckled softly. "It *was* a lifetime ago. Funny thing is, he didn't act like he'd ever met me when he checked in here."

"Seriously? How did you know him? From where?" I leaned my elbow on the table and cupped my chin in my hand.

"Oh, years ago, back in my youth. I got a job in the city as a secretary at an investing firm. It was Mr. Green's family's firm, and he'd just started working there himself." She smiled as she weaved a lattice across the pie top. "We were both so young."

"Really. Did you like him?"

"Oh, he'd seemed so sophisticated and ambitious, like all those young investors are. Everything was about the killer instinct and making money. We actually went out to dinner once." Her smile flickered again. "Maybe twice."

I straightened up. Cecelia had dated Mr. Green? "Once or twice? Once means he struck out. Twice means you liked him a bit."

"Maybe a few times more than that," she finally conceded with a laugh.

I covered my mouth, half incredulous. "I don't even know where to put that."

"Well, it fizzled out. I moved out this way, met Gerald, and the rest was history." She started to crimp the edge of the pie crust. "Like I said. It was a long time ago."

She dusted her hands on her apron, and then checked the temperature on the oven. Satisfied, she carefully lifted the pie and slid it into the oven.

A man's shouts rang through the house. I rolled my eyes. "I've got it," I told her, and went to track it down.

It wasn't hard to find the source. I could hear the men arguing in the living room all the way down the hall. I walked inside to discover the St. Claires sitting together on the couch, while Mr. Peterson, Eliza Sue, and Sarah sat in the armchairs. The coffee table in the center of the group was strewn with cards.

"Don't go there," Mr. Peterson said. He stared hard at Mr. St. Claire.

I wasn't sure if I should interrupt. I sidled over into one of the empty wing chairs to watch.

"What's the matter? You got a problem again? Want to fold?" Mr. St. Claire's voice held joviality that his eyes belied. They stared like sharp pieces of black flint behind his glasses.

Around the table, the other guests shifted, nervous to suddenly be caught in the unexpected crossfire of two egos.

Mr. Peterson held his stare. "You know what I'm talking about. I said don't go there, or I will."

Mr. St. Claire smiled, a smile that sent shivers down my spine. A smile that was threatening, teeth bared, eyes narrowed. "Sounds like something's bothering you, son. Why don't you tell us what it is?"

Mr. Peterson drew back in his chair. His eyes narrowed as if considering if Mr. St. Claire really meant his words. I could almost see the wheels turning in his head. Was Mr. Peterson about to confront him about the conversation he'd heard outside their window last night? "You're calling my bluff?"

Mr. St. Claire's smile didn't waver. He calmly flipped over a card. "Oh, look. I've got an Ace. Your call."

I could have sworn everyone held their breath, waiting for the next move.

"Well, I'm out," Sarah said, throwing her cards onto the table.

"Honey..." Mrs. St. Claire grabbed her husband's arm. Ever so subtly, he shrugged her off.

Mr. Peterson tapped his card against the table. Tap. Tap. Tap.

"You going to call me or what?" Mr. St. Claire asked.

Mr. Peterson relaxed and gave his characteristic wink. "Not this time, buddy. I fold."

"That's what I figured," Mr. St. Claire said. He scooped the pile of dollar bills in the center of the table toward him.

Mr. Peterson stood and pulled a cigarette from his pocket. He calmly lit it.

"Hey! You can't smoke in here," Eliza Sue said.

He ignored her, his eyes squinting against the smoke as he inhaled. The coal on the end of the cigarette glowed red. He removed the cigarette from his mouth and pointed it at Mr. St. Claire. "I'm surprised you forgot that we've met before." Smoke streamed from his nostrils.

Mr. St. Claire froze, his hand still on the pile of money.

"Don't you remember? It was at Chuckie's place. Brooklyn."

"Jared?" Mrs. St. Claire looked at her husband with her brow wrinkled. She'd somehow found time to put her makeup on, and her heavily blue-shadowed eyes were wide with worry.

Mr. St. Claire nudged his glasses and shook his head slightly to silence her. Slowly, he gathered the cards from around the table. I tried not to shiver as I noticed the back of his hand was covered in scrapes.

"Wasn't me. Never been to Brooklyn. Sorry, buddy." His face was expressionless. With a ruffling noise, he began to reshuffle the deck.

"No?" Mr. Peterson's eyebrows arched with doubt. "Must be my mistake then." He pulled his phone from his pocket, which was buzzing mightily. After a glance at it, he stood up.

"Well, looky here. I've been summoned to the police station. I guess I'll see the rest of you later." With a wink at me, he headed out the front door.

CHAPTER 10

"So they're actually calling us down, I guess," Eliza Sue said glumly.

The St. Claires both spoke at the same time, with Mr. St. Claire winning out. "This is ridiculous. I have work on Monday."

"You forget. We'd planned to visit my parents," Mrs. St. Claire reminded him with a look.

"Mm." He lifted an eyebrow. "Darn. Looks like we'll be missing out on that."

"They've been looking forward to it. Don't act that way!" she snapped back. Her face flushed, matching her hair, and her eyes narrowed.

"Hey, can I help it if we're being detained for questioning?" he answered with a shrug. He blocked her swat.

"Well I, for one, have plans," Sarah interrupted.

The fighting couple stared at each other for a moment longer. Seeing she didn't have their attention, Sarah continued a little louder. "Yeah, I have to get going myself. I've missed my cross-fit training for weeks, and I have a job interview on Monday. Seems really unnecessary."

"Not exactly unnecessary," Eliza Sue said softly. "I mean, Mr. Green *is* dead. Murdered. And we were all there."

I blinked, surprised to hear Eliza Sue address the situation so bluntly. From the coughs and shifting around the table, I think we all were.

"What?" she asked, looking around at us. "It's true."

"Just because we were all there doesn't mean one of us is the murderer," Mr. St. Claire said. He nudged his glasses up his nose.

"Oh, really?" Eliza Sue said. "I'd love to hear this."

"I mean...." He glanced around at us as if for help. "It could have been anybody."

"Anybody with a knife? It wasn't anybody. It was one of us." She sharply stabbed her index finger at each one of us.

Mrs. St. Claire flinched as though really stabbed. "I don't believe it."

"Explain to me what happened then?" Eliza Sue asked.

"Someone could have snuck in." Mrs. St. Claire's tongue dabbed at what appeared to be a very dry lip.

"Snuck. In." Eliza Sue's face was deadpan.

"Yes. Snuck in. And disappeared in the commotion. It was dark down there," Mrs. St. Claire said defensively.

"And the flash did blind us," Mr. St. Claire added. He put his arm around his wife's shoulders.

"And he could have disappeared while we were all focused on poor Mr. Green," Sarah interjected, cracking her knuckles.

Just then, the front door opened. Mrs. Green walked by the dining room entrance, with her dad's arm protectively around her. Normally, the blonde woman walked with a wealthy confidence, her head high, but now she walked as though deflated with grief. Behind them trailed her mother, who paused outside the living room doorway.

"We're just going to get her packed up and get ready to leave," Mrs. Green's mother explained.

"Do you need any help?" I asked.

She shook her head, and then quickly followed after her family. Their footsteps were muffled on the hall rug. Seconds later, a door opened, and then shut with a click.

"Why does she get to leave, anyway?" Mr. St. Claire said defensively.

"Shh," Mrs. St. Claire said, leaning forward. As she did, a red wave of hair slipped out of her clip and fell across her cheek. "She's the grieving widow. She has to get back to wherever they've sent her husband. She has arrangements to make."

"Since when does being the wife let you off from being a suspect?" Mr. St. Claire said bitterly.

"Jared! How could you?" his wife exclaimed.

Eliza Sue tipped her head and opened her hands. "That is true."

I sighed and rubbed my temple. There wasn't going to be enough coffee to get me through this morning.

"What about that lady? The one who ran around talking about ghosts?" Sarah asked.

"Why on earth would the curator want to kill Mr. Green?" Mrs. St. Claire asked, her eyebrows raised incredulously.

Mr. St. Claire scratched at his stubbly chin. "Why would any of us?"

The house phone rang, making us all jump. I think it'd been a while since any of us heard anything but a cell phone sound off in a while. I heard Cecelia answer it in the kitchen. Her voice was low as she said, "Okay, I'll let them know," and hung up.

Seconds later, she appeared in the dining room. "That was Sheriff Parker. He'd like the rest of you to go ahead and go down to the precinct now. There are officers there ready to take your official statements."

CHAPTER 11

"*I* can drive you guys down," I said and stood up.

Mr. St. Claire looked at his wife. His nostrils flared. "I'm waiting to hear back from our lawyer."

Lawyer? I thought about that for a second, considering whether I should call one myself. It did make sense. But who would I call?

"Don't freak out. It's just a statement," Eliza Sue said. "If things get squirrely, then you can bring your lawyer into it."

"Just a statement, huh?" Sarah rolled her eyes.

"Seriously. You guys worrying about it is making me worried about *you*," Eliza Sue snapped back.

I cleared my throat to get everyone's attention. "Anyone want a ride? I'm heading down there right now."

"I'll go with you," Eliza Sue said. "Just let me grab a few things." She quickly left the room.

"Me, too," Sarah said. She gulped the last few sips of her coffee and then stood up.

"I'm waiting for my lawyer to call back," Mr. St. Claire said stubbornly. "You guys should, too."

"I'll keep that in mind," I answered, but in reality I knew I couldn't afford a lawyer. It'd be a court-appointed attorney for me. I bit back a groan and opened my purse for my keys. I shook it a bit. There they were at the bottom, giving a reassuring jingle.

Cecelia nudged my arm. "Do you suppose they want Mrs. Green, too?" she whispered.

I winced but nodded.

"Of course they do," she answered herself. She reached back to untie her apron. "I'll go let her know."

As I turned to leave the living room, I caught a glimpse of my face in the curio cabinet mirror. The wet brush didn't do the trick this morning. My hair was a mess. I tried to smooth it back, and ignore the dark circles under my green eyes. It was obvious that I didn't do well with little sleep. Walking toward the door, I pinched my cheeks to add a little color, and headed outside.

The temperature was falling, and I could see my breath in the air. I wondered if we wouldn't be getting snow by the nightfall.

I trotted down the porch steps, noticing more cigarette butts littering the ground. *This place is going to need a thorough going-over from the gardens on up.* Shaking my head, I started toward the van when I noticed a yellow piece of paper caught in one of the rose bushes.

Garbage everywhere. I walked over, the driveway gravel crunching under my feet. Carefully, I untangled the paper from the thorns. I was about to crumple it up, but curiosity made me check it first.

The paper was so worn it was soft. I gently smoothed it out. It read:

The butcher, the baker,

The candlestick maker.

Turn them out, knaves all three.

Hm. Just some children's poem. I folded it up and stuck it into my pocket. *Now where are those ladies?* I climbed up into Old Bella and immediately spritzed the air freshener, slightly disappointed that the cold air hadn't squashed the barbecue scent today.

I started the van to let it warm up. It chugged and rumbled as it tried to find its idle. Mr. Peterson's earlier words were on my mind, along with how adamant Mr. St. Claire had been about getting a lawyer. Did Mr. Peterson know him? Was it possible the reason Mr. St. Claire was so adamant about a lawyer was for more than just common sense?

I stared out toward the main road. Cecelia really had an amazing piece of property. Huge stately maple trees darkened the edge of the driveway. They were so old, they'd probably seen horse-drawn carriages come down this way. The few leaves left on the maples shivered in the breeze.

Sarah opened the sliding door. "You ready?"

I nodded. "As ready as I'll ever be. Should be interesting."

"Do you think Rachel will join us?"

I shook my head. "Her parents can drive her."

The front door slammed and Eliza Sue came down the steps. She had on capris and a thick jacket. On her feet, she wore what my aunt would call sensible shoes—white sneakers with a little blue tag on the back. Her socks were pulled high up thick, shiny calves.

"Sorry to keep you guys waiting. I needed to change," she said as she climbed in. She sat next to Sarah with a thump and slid the door closed.

"All right, folks. Here we go," I said. We buckled up and I drove out into the road.

"What sorts of questions do you think they'll ask?" Sarah's voice came from the back. I glanced in the rearview mirror and caught sight of her anxious face, her forehead lined with wrinkles like notebook paper.

"Probably similar to the ones Sheriff Parker asked last night." Eliza Sue coughed. "Oh. That's right. You went to bed and didn't see him."

"He was here last night?" Sarah sounded surprised.

"Yeah. Just asking one more time where everyone was in the hallway. I said you were next to me." Eliza Sue tacked the last thought on.

I wondered about that for a moment, realizing I had no idea where Sarah had actually been that night.

The silence stretched out. Then Sarah broke it by saying, "I wasn't though. I was standing by Mr. St. Claire when someone pushed me."

I tried to remember exactly where I'd been in the line-up. We'd gone down the stairs, Mrs. Stilton leading the way. It was nearly pitch black. I thought the Greens had been behind her, and then everyone else. And then there had been me, like the caboose behind them all.

But when we got to the hallway and there was still no light, we kind of all crowded together. It was a jumble, for sure. I remembered Mrs. Stilton shouting for us to wait just a minute so she could turn on the light.

And then the explosion.

"Did Sheriff Parker ever say what caused the breaker to do that?" I asked as I turned down another street. It might've been a while since I last lived here, but I knew exactly where the police department was. As did almost every high school senior, who at one point or another was caught doing something they shouldn't be and brought there to wait for their parents. Grandma had not been too happy when she'd picked me up. Or so she led me to believe. After she'd banished me to my room for what she thought was a suitable amount of time, she confessed with a chuckle that she'd had to pick my mom up from there too.

Kind of made me proud I'd followed in my mom's footsteps.

"The cause of the explosion? Yeah, he did explain it," Eliza Sue answered. "He said the overhead light bulb had been unscrewed just enough to lose its connection. And that someone had *tampered* with the hall lamp."

"I'll say they tampered with it," I mumbled, remembering the blast. But her words sent ice through my veins. This proved it was premeditated murder.

CHAPTER 12

We arrived at the precinct, just a small building with a big name in our little town. After exchanging phone numbers in case one of us should be done first, we headed inside. The officer at the front desk had the three of us sit on a wooden bench outside one of the offices.

"Sheriff Parker knows you're here. He'll have someone come get you shortly," the officer said.

I looked around. It was no different from when I'd last been here at seventeen. The bench was uncomfortable, and the air stifling. Dirty smudges stood out on the bare walls from the bright overhead fluorescent lighting. The linoleum floor was worn to a gray streak down the middle from years of foot traffic. I glanced at Sarah and Eliza Sue. The two women appeared just as bored as I felt. With a deep breath, I pulled out my phone to do some web surfing.

There was something I was kind of curious about. Watching Cecelia make that pie kind of piqued my interest. Were all pies that hard to make? Was this something someone like me —a complete novice—could ever do? The search page opened up to a variety of fruit pies. I clicked the recipe for cherry pie. As I read it, my stomach growled.

"You ready, young lady?" A voice broke my concentration. Sheriff Parker had come out of his office and now stared down at me. Gruff, and in his late fifties, his paunch hung over his belt.

I nodded and rose to follow him, tucking my phone into my purse.

His office was cold and his desk messy. I took a chair across from him and waited.

"So." He pushed over a piece of paper and a pencil. "Using initials, can you make circles and mark where everyone was when the lamp exploded?"

I took the paper and did my best. It was hard to remember. By the time I was done, Mr. Green was in the center of our group. Any one of us could have stabbed him.

He raised an eyebrow as he examined it. "Helpful," he said dryly.

"I'm sorry," I answered, biting my lip. "It's the best I can remember."

He sighed, his large nostrils flaring. "Do you have any idea what caused the explosion?"

I shook my head.

"It was a penny. Officer Wagner uncovered it."

Frank had? "A... penny?"

"Specifically, a wheat penny. It was blown nearly in half, but enough of it remained to identify it. Do you know what that is?"

I nodded, familiar with that design. It was something I'd loved to collect as a kid, along with a stamp collection. But I hadn't seen one in a long while.

"Pretty rare. Not too many in circulation anymore." He grabbed the pencil and tapped it against the desk. The interview finished with him asking me if I'd seen anything I thought was unusual, to which I answered no.

"Just like I'm telling everyone, stay in town the next few days. We might need to ask you a few more questions."

I nodded, and after promising I'd come to him if I thought of anything else, I left his office.

Mrs. Stilton was sitting on the bench when I was released from the interview. "I'm so glad to see you!"

I was slightly caught off guard, seeing her in her street clothes.

"Hi, Mrs. Stilton. Wow, you look different without the hat."

She felt her hair—now unpinned and hanging below her shoulders—and laughed. "Please, call me Leslie. I kind of miss my hat. Makes it easy to get ready in the morning."

As I nodded, she patted a bag next to her. I immediately recognized it. Eliza Sue's paper bag, complete with the large water bottle sticking out from the top.

"Oh, wow!" I said, accepting the bag. "Where did you find it?"

"In the basement. She must have forgotten it in the horror of that night." Her lips turned down sadly. "I almost sent it home with two of your guests who just left the station. But they were so chummy together, I didn't want to disturb them. Besides, I thought I'd better give it to you personally."

"Chummy? Who just left?"

"That one young woman left with the tall man."

I nodded. That must have been Sarah and Mr. Peterson.

An officer called Mrs. Stilton to the back room. I waved as she left, and headed out to the van.

As I was leaving the building, the St. Claires arrived, accompanied by a rather somber-looking man.

"Nice day for an interview," I said teasingly. I shouldn't have said it—needling Mr. St. Claire like that—but that entitlement of his irked me. I was rewarded with a sour look from Mr. St. Claire.

All righty, then. At least I didn't have to deal with them for too much longer. Once in the van, I sent a text to Eliza Sue, letting her know where I was, and then searched up the wheat penny that Sheriff Parker had mentioned.

The browser opened to images of the penny. I'd seen the coin before, but he was right. It had been a long time.

My phone buzzed with a text, letting me know Eliza Sue was on her way out.

Perfect timing. I was ready to get out of here. And after looking at all those pies, I was starving.

She opened the passenger door and climbed in with a sigh.

"How'd it go?" I asked, trying to read her body language.

"Fine. But I swear, I'm more tired than I've been in a long

time." The fortyish-year-old woman's face attested to that exhaustion, looking like a flower in desperate need of watering.

"I hear you. Well, I don't know about you, Ms. Eliza Sue, but I'm ready for some food. Want to go get something to eat?"

She glanced at me as if wondering if I were trying to trick her.

"You want to go out to eat? Why?" She honestly appeared puzzled.

"Well, because I'm hungry. Aren't you? Let's just go grab a bite. We don't have to talk about anything serious."

She studied me, the lines between her eyebrows deepening. Her nostrils widened as she exhaled. Finally, she nodded, almost as if I were offering her a punishment.

I frowned at her reaction. "You don't have to go, if you don't want to. I can just drop you back at the bed and breakfast."

"A body's got to eat, doesn't it?" She buckled up. "And mine's in the mood for tacos."

I laughed and started Old Bella up. "Sounds good to me. I know just the place. There's a taco truck down by the car dealership on the west end of town."

We drove through the historical part of Gainesville.

"You see that building over there?" I pointed.

She looked and nodded.

"They used to sell everything. And one of the things they sold was overalls. The thickest denim overalls you've ever seen. They were practically indestructible. My grandma loved them. I swear that's all I wore clear through the fifth grade."

"Really?" She giggled.

"Yeah."

"What changed in sixth grade?"

"Boys," I said simply. "I noticed boys and I saw that overalls were like an invisibility cloak. One I didn't want any more."

She chuckled again.

I turned onto a side street. After following that for a few blocks, we came to the more commercial side of town. The modern businesses were housed in buildings built in a mock appearance of the 1800's. I loved how our town did everything to preserve its historical flavor.

Outside the grocery store—built out of red brick and with a long awning—was the taco truck. This sat on an open gravel area off to the side of the store's parking lot. There were three picnic benches next to it under portable awnings. The tables were partially filled. Only one had a single customer, so Eliza Sue and I took our tacos over.

We sat down on opposite sides of the picnic table. The other person gave us a smile before looking down at her phone. I unwrapped my food while Eliza Sue took a sip of her soda. She glanced around for a moment, before saying, "You know, this is only my second vacation in my adult life."

"What?" I'd just taken a big bite and hurriedly chewed.

"I mean it," she answered. "I was the head assistant at an accounting business for the last seventeen years."

"They didn't give you vacation?"

She shrugged. Her shoulders rounded and brought to my mind a pack animal that had been worked too long.

"They did. I just didn't want a vacation."

"Why on earth not?"

"It's easy for you to ask that," she snapped. "You're cute. Well liked. You have people around you all the time. I have no one. So it didn't seem like too much fun to sit at home for a week staring at the same four walls that I came to work to escape."

I took a sip of my soda, not wanting to respond until the sting of her comment faded. She didn't think I could understand loneliness?

Derek came to mind.

CHERRY PIE OR DIE

A lump formed in my throat, and I swallowed. Not today, and not in front of her. She wasn't worthy of my true feelings.

"So what did you do on your first vacation?" I asked as way of distraction.

She'd just taken a bite and cupped her hand over her mouth as she chewed. After a moment, she answered, "I went to Tampa, Florida. That was my first time out of state." She wrinkled her nose. "Too much skin showing. Of all ages."

"Where are you from again?"

"New Jersey," she said. She carefully plucked a piece of lettuce from the front of her shirt.

"This vacation hasn't been that great either, huh?" I said.

"Oh, it was fine, up until Mr. Green died." She looked at me. "Although I think Rachel is faking it."

My mouth fell open. "Faking what?"

"Her grief. That woman was about as into her husband as a vegan into a greasy hamburger. He repelled her, I swear."

I could hardly believe she said that. So coldly, like she hadn't actually been comforting the woman last night and this morning. And bringing her clothes. What was going on?

"I'm really surprised to hear you say that," I said, trying to carefully pick my words. "You seemed incredibly supportive this morning." I tried my best to keep cool, but it was hard. This was striking too close to home for me.

She sighed. "When you get to be my age you realize people have two sides. One side they want to pretend they are, and the other which is who they really are. Rachel wants to be a shocked, grieving widow. She's doing her best to play that part. But you weren't around at night to see the way they talked to each other. He obviously chose her to be his trophy wife. And she was a gold digger. You know what they say about gold diggers? You marry for money, you pay for the rest of your life." She took another sip of her soda.

I blinked hard. "How do you know all of this. And if you thought it, why would you be nice to her?"

"Well, I wanted to give her a chance. After all, I don't know her. Just basing my opinions on what I heard. He really wasn't kind to her. Every morning was the same thing. He'd say, 'You're going to wear that? Don't wear that. Go put on the pink shirt I got you. You're going to eat that?' And then there's what happened the night before our tour."

I almost didn't want to ask, because I didn't want to encourage her line of thought. But curiosity got to me. "What happened the night before?"

"They got into the most horrific argument. You know how my

room is right next to theirs. Well, I could hear every word. He was screaming." She shivered.

"Screaming what?"

Eliza Sue glanced to the side to see if the girl at the end of the table was paying attention. Then she leaned over and whispered, "He said, 'I told you no kids. That was the rule.' And then she started crying."

"And?" I held my breath.

"And he said, 'It's not mine. You know that.'"

My back stiffened. "'It's not mine,' like..."

"Exactly." Eliza Sue raised her eyebrows. "Have you seen her eat anything lately?"

I frowned, remembering the comment she'd made at my house about how little she'd eaten that day. Obviously, no one could expect her to eat with the shock and grief. A loss of appetite was normal. I remember barely eating for two weeks after Derek died. "No, but after what happened..."

"Grieving, right?" She smirked. "It gives a good excuse to not eat. Which is helpful when you don't want to explain morning sickness." She took another bite and calmly waited for my response.

I rubbed the back of my neck. "And you heard Mr. Green say it wasn't his."

"About a million times. Shouted it practically from the rafters. But I have an idea whose it is." Her eyes glinted mischievously.

"Who?"

She shrugged coyly and kept chewing. Seriously? She was going to drop that bomb and not tell me?

"Did she admit she was pregnant?"

"No. Mr. Green said they'd be taking a test when they got back. And if it was positive, it was over. He wanted a divorce. He was very clear about that. 'Two pink lines means your meal ticket is over, Missy. It's back to waitressing for you.'"

I thought about Rachel, blonde and beautiful, all bedecked in her Fendi wallet, Birkin bag, and Louis Vuitton shoes. That would be a hard step down for her to take.

But, with the life insurance, now it would be a step she wouldn't have to take.

CHAPTER 13

I turned down Baker Street, relieved to be back at the bed and breakfast. Lunch had been informative, but I was ready for a break.

"You have any plans for today?" I asked Eliza Sue, after I parked.

She opened the door. "No, I think I'm due for a little nap. But I want you to think about what I said."

Watching her climb out jolted my memory. "Hey, I have something for you."

"Yeah? What is it?" she asked. The suspicious cast came to her eyes again.

"Your jacket and water bottle. Mrs. Stilton gave them to me at the station." I reached into the back seat for the bag.

Seeing the bag, her face broke into a huge smile. "Oh, my goodness! I forgot about it with the craziness of that night. My favorite water bottle, actually. I got it from my boss on my fifteen-year anniversary there."

I passed the bag over.

"Hi, Georgie," a voice called from the porch.

I glanced up to see Rachel Green standing on the top step. She had on worn jeans and a buttoned top, a more casual look than I'd seen her in before. Eliza Sue gave her a cool hello as she passed by to walk inside.

"What are you still doing here?" I asked Rachel. I glanced around but didn't see her parents' Lincoln. "I thought you were going home with your mom and dad."

"Oh, they just ran to the store. Probably needed a minute away from mopey ol' me," she said with a sad smile.

I walked up the steps toward her. "Nonsense. You aren't mopey. Actually, you are handling all of this a lot better than I ever—" I swallowed, not wanting to add the word, "did." I didn't want to follow that word with an explanation, so I hurried with the next question. "How are you feeling today?"

She gave a weak shrug that broke my heart.

"It's okay to not be okay. You're going to feel like half a person for a while. I know it's hard, and you might not be able to see your way to the end, but you will eventually find yourself. But for now, live in the memories. Give yourself permission to feel however you need to feel."

Her bottom lip trembled, but she stiffened her chin and nodded. "Right now, I think I need a break from feelings. They're like tsunami waves, and there's been no escape."

I listened. Was this emotion real, or was it the person she wanted to be, like Eliza Sue said.

"Anyway," she continued, "I'm here now, so..."

"When was the last time you had something to eat?" I asked.

She shrugged.

"Want me to go make you something?"

Rachel shook her head. "No, I'm not really hungry."

"How about hot cocoa? Tea?"

"Fine. I'll take a cup of tea. Mint, maybe?"

"You got it." We walked inside together, and I left her heading toward the living room as I walked into the kitchen.

Cecelia's pie was cooling on the counter. Next to it was a rack filled with scones. Oh, man. I could just taste one with Cecelia's fresh raspberry—

"You take that back, you wench!" a woman screamed from the living room. I stood with my hand frozen over the scones. The woman's voice got louder and her language saltier.

Now what? These guys are worse than a group of toddlers strung out on sugar, fighting over the last teddy bear. I ran for the living room.

I entered to see the group scattered about on various chairs and sofas. Eliza Sue was standing by the fireplace, her arms crossed before her. Standing near the window, Mr. Peterson rubbed the back of his neck like he had a tattoo he was trying to erase. Mrs. St. Claire perched on the claw-footed couch with her arm around the shoulders of Rachel. I couldn't see Rachel's face; it was buried in her hands.

Sarah stood by the sideboard, dumbly looking down at the decanters.

After a moment, Mr. Peterson walked over to her. "I could use a drink, myself."

Sarah stared up at him, her eyes darkly lined with mascara, making them stand out on an otherwise pale face.

"You want something?" he asked her, uncorking the decanter. "Apparently, as the player, I should ask." When she silently nodded, he grabbed two shot glasses and poured a couple of fingers full.

She took the glass from him. He threw his shot back, and with a grimace, poured another. This time he held it up like a cheers to the rest of us, before knocking it back.

"What's going on?" I asked, not at all sure I wanted to hear the answer.

"Well," Mr. Peterson began with a wry grin. "Apparently Eliza Sue can't take a joke, and I've only just discovered I'm part of a love triangle I knew nothing about."

"He tried to call me a liar." Eliza Sue's eyebrows made two angry slashes like some cartoon figures.

"Nonsense," Mr. Peterson corrected. "I called you a know-it-all. It seems I was wrong. What I should have said was a hot-aired loony-tune gossip." He held up the whiskey. Light flashed off the etched decanter. "Anyone else?" he asked.

No one responded. Tension was thick in the air.

Eliza Sue shook her head so hard her dark curls swayed. "Don't you be denying it. You know!" She pointed her finger at him. "You know I saw you that night. You're trying to make me sound crazy!"

My skin prickled. Was this what Eliza Sue meant earlier when she said she had an idea who the father was?

"You saw me?" He arched an eyebrow.

"Yes. You and Rachel. You two were coming back through the yard. And Michael Green came out of the back door. You jumped into the maple tree and climbed up. He almost caught the two of you." Her hand was shaking with indignation. She spun around to face Rachel. "And you said, 'Oh, honey, I just needed some air. I thought you were asleep.'"

"If you thought this about me, why did you try to help me?" Rachel wailed.

"I was watching you to see if you'd slip up. I wasn't sure what to think yet. I knew he wasn't pleasant to you. And I knew you had...problems." Eliza Sue's gaze cut to Rachel's midsection.

"Like I said, that sounds like the ravings of a lunatic," Mr. Peterson said mildly. And then, to me, "That never happened."

Sarah took a small sip from her shot glass. "You did say you saw her the other night."

"That's right. I saw her. We talked about how bright the moon was." He nodded emphatically. He reached out to touch her elbow. "Sarah?"

Sarah stiffened and slowly walked over to the couch.

"Well, I for one am not going to stand for this," Mrs. St. Claire said. "I think you are a stroppy cow, Eliza Sue! How dare you accuse Rachel like this."

"Sorry it bothered you, but I'm telling the truth," Eliza Sue said.

"The truth? You come in here spouting accusations of her cheating on Mr. Green. And for what?" Mrs. St. Claire said. She flipped her red hair impatiently over her shoulder. "Maybe that came from jealousy, hmm? Maybe you wish you had someone interested in you."

I glanced again at Eliza Sue and was horrified to see her actually puffing up, as if she were a blowfish. Her chest went out, and her chin dipped. I braced myself for her response.

It wasn't quite as spectacular as I expected, but still passion-infused.

"How dare you. How *dare* you!" Eliza Sue sputtered. Her face turned red, making her eyes seem even beadier. She turned to me and yelled, "Are you just going to stand there and let her talk to me that way?"

My mouth dropped open. What was I, the teacher? I shook my head. "What do you want me to say?"

"What's the matter, Eliza Sue? You can't fight your own battles? You're just one to drop mean accusations and run?

Well, let me tell you, that isn't happening around me anymore." Mrs. St. Claire was smiling now. Not a nice smile, but one that meant she thought she was winning.

Eliza Sue stomped out of the room. Her steps echoed from the stairs.

Mrs. St. Claire's lips were still curled in a grin. "Rachel, don't worry. No one took her seriously."

Rachel's blonde head hung low, but she was no longer covering her face.

Her husband added, "Don't worry, Rachel. No one believes her. She's a bitter old—"

Sarah snorted and knocked back the rest of her drink. I thought she was going to respond. Instead, she glared at Mr. Peterson before slamming the glass down on the coffee table. She stormed out.

Mr. St. Claire studied the glass on the table and then turned toward Mr. Peterson. "Well, I'll say this. You seem to stir up trouble wherever you go."

Mr. Peterson's mouth moved like he was about to tell him off. Instead, he set his glass down carefully. "Well folks, this has been fun. With that, I bid you adieu." He gave us a small salute, and left the room to saunter up the stairs.

Mr. St. Claire pushed his glasses up his nose. "And you, my

little wife. Red temper to match your hair. You just had to jump right in the middle, huh? You sure upset Eliza Sue."

Mrs. St. Claire patted Rachel's arm sympathetically. "I couldn't handle her gleeful smirks after she dropped the gold-digger bomb. It was ridiculous, but it hurt Rachel. I'm not letting that go down on my watch. Besides, if Eliza Sue really was upset, where were her tears when she stormed off 'crying'?"

Rachel smiled gratefully at her friend.

"You okay?" Mrs. St. Claire asked, patting her shoulder.

"I'm okay. Just very, very drained." Rachel's face seemed to appear even more drawn down with that word. "I think I'm going to go lie down until my parents get here."

We all gave soft encouragements for her to rest. She wearily walked down the hall to her room.

Mrs. St. Claire looked at me.

"Looks like everyone's run off," Mr. St. Claire said. He grabbed the deck of cards on the coffee table and slowly shuffled them. "You in?" he asked me.

"Jared!" Mrs. St. Claire exclaimed. "How can you just change the subject like that?"

"Like what? Everyone's upset. I, on the other hand, had a long morning at the police station, and now I'm ready to relax and play some blackjack."

"Blackjack? I have no idea how to play that," I said.

"You got some cash? Cause now's the time to learn."

I arched an eyebrow and he laughed.

Mrs. St. Claire rolled her eyes and then slumped back into the couch. She blew out a deep breath. "I'm actually kind of disappointed Eliza Sue left. I was ready for a fight."

"A fight?" Mr. St. Claire asked. He side-eyed her as he dealt the cards.

"She got me going, and I was ready to call her out. But she just ran away like a wimp."

"I'd call that a win," her husband said, passing her cards.

Mrs. St. Claire accepted them and fanned them in her hand. "Please. That was hardly a fight. She has no idea how bloody I can get."

CHAPTER 14

"Everything okay in here?" Cecelia appeared in the doorway, wiping her hands on a dishtowel.

"Just peachy!" Mr. St. Claire called.

I took her appearance as a life line and walked in her direction. It really had been a long day, and I didn't think now would be the time to learn a card game. Especially one for money. I remembered how Frank took all my collectors cards when we bet on Hearts. It'd been the first time I'd played it, and it hadn't gone well.

Of course, I got my revenge by winning them all back when we'd bet on who would catch the first fish of the season. He hadn't stood a chance.

We walked into the kitchen, where I started on the remainder of the lunch dishes. Cecelia's brow furrowed with worry, and I felt her customary three pats on my back, her way of checking to make sure I was okay. I smiled to reassure her everything was fine.

I washed in silence, stacking them in the dish drainer, and then dried my hands on a towel. "I think I'm going to head home for a bit, if you don't mind."

"Of course not. But come back for dinner. I planned a little family meal." Her gaze flicked to the kitchen table where we sometimes ate separately from the guests.

"Everyone eating out tonight?" I asked.

"As far as I know, everyone has plans. Eliza Sue, you know, usually takes her evening walk. I don't think poor Rachel will be here. As for the rest, I'm surprised they haven't scattered yet."

Well, I knew why they hadn't scattered. Originally, we had an exploration of another old cemetery scheduled for today. But with everything that had happened, along with this morning's trip to the police station, it seemed very inappropriate.

"Anyway, as long as you're going home, will you drop this off next door, first?" Cecelia turned to the counter, where there sat a big wedge of pie on one of her china plates. It was already covered in saran wrap and a red-checked cloth napkin.

I picked it up, hoping I'd heard her wrong. "Take it where?"

"You know, to Oscar. Mr. O'Neil. To kind of make up for what happened this morning. You said he had a run-in with Mr. Peterson. I know Oscar doesn't come off that way, but he really is a kind man. I want to make it up to him."

Oh, that's right. Wow, this morning felt like a lifetime ago. Her comment of "nice man" didn't exactly blend with my experience. I eyed the pie.

Cecelia smiled sweetly. Inwardly, I groaned. I couldn't tell her no. *Suck it up, buttercup.* I grinned back. "You got it."

"Thank you, dear," she said. "And if he doesn't answer, just knock harder. He's hard of hearing."

I have to admit, the thought of pounding on an angry neighbor's door didn't exactly fill me with sunny thoughts. I just hoped he wouldn't answer with a shot gun. I grabbed the plate and waved at the St. Claires as I passed.

The plate was warm in my hand, the pie still clinging to the last vestiges of heat from the oven. The crust was flaky, with a few syrupy cherries oozing to the side. It definitely was a fair peace offering for the cigarette butt earlier.

I cut across the lawn and walked down his driveway. His empty trash can had blown over. I righted it and found its lid. Apprehension curled in my gut as I stared at the house.

No shutters, no blinds, not a single curtain. All the windows stared back dark and lifeless. Even from here, I could see the white paint on the siding severely needed to be redone.

Squaring my shoulders, I marched up to the porch. At the base of the steps were several old phonebooks that had been delivered at one point. The pages had swelled with rain water.

I climbed the stairs. Paint peeled off the railing in white, razor-like shards. The boards creaked under my feet. A nearly leafless wisteria bush climbed the side of the railings, its vines aggressively pulling at the slats.

A spider web brushed my face, and I jumped, nearly upsetting the pie. I quickly made my way to the entrance.

"Hello?" I tapped on the door. A glance around the porch revealed a decrepit rocker, a broken pot still half filled with dirt, and enough piled up newspapers to fill several recycling bins.

"Who is it?" a grouchy voice yelled from inside. It was the same voice that had yelled at us earlier, and my imagination started to run wild again with pictures of a shotgun.

I swallowed and held the piece of pie before me like a shield. "I've got a pie from Cecelia Wagner. She asked me to bring it over to you."

There was shuffling and then the loud sound of something falling and hitting the wood floor. I tensed, but it hadn't sounded heavy enough to be a person.

Seconds later, the lock clanked back and the door opened a crack. One glaring eye framed by a crazy white eyebrow appeared in the gap of the doorway.

"What do you want?" he growled.

I pushed forward the plate. "Here. For you." It seemed my grasp of communication had vanished at his appearance. I straightened my shoulders and said, a little clearer, "I'm Georgie Tanner. I work for Cecelia. She's been baking and wanted you to have this. As an apology for one of our guests."

The eye glared down at the pie. He grumbled and shuffled back. The door opened some more, showing a man in a ratty red sweatshirt and striped pajama bottoms. Worn slippers were on his feet. His hair stuck up in the back as if he'd just woken up.

He turned and left the doorway. I hesitated. Did he want me to follow him? With my finger, I pushed the door open a bit more. He was already halfway down the dark hallway, heading for what I presumed was the living room.

What I was not prepared for was the white blur that shot past him and toward me. Pie still in air, I danced around the little dog barking shrilly at my ankles.

Mr. O'Neil acted like he didn't hear a thing. Just kept on going, leaving me to deal with the white hooligan.

"Shh!" I said. "You're okay, girl. Boy? Shh. Good boy. Good girl."

The puffy dog seemed to simmer down at my feet and stared up at me. At least, I assumed the animal was staring at me. The fur fell to the bridge of its nose like an avalanche of snow.

"Peanut!" Mr. O'Neil yelled. The dog took off running in his direction. Okay, then. I followed, glancing around and feeling like a house intruder casing a joint. Well, that was partly true. I was definitely checking things out, but there was nothing here I'd want to take.

I walked down the hall, past an army of family photos that hung on the wall. A woman with white curly hair and a sweet smile was in more than a few. As I walked the wall's length, her hair grew longer, darker, and the lines on her face disappeared. At the end, she sat in a chair with two little boys and a young version of Mr. O'Neil.

It was sad how you could pass a person's whole life with just a few steps down a dimly-lit hallway. A lump grew in my throat. Great. Not only would I have to show bravado, I'd have to do it sounding like Kermit the Frog.

I entered the living room just as Mr. O'Neil settled with a wheeze into an old velour easy chair.

"Where would you like me to put this?" I asked, glancing around. The room looked like a Hallmark store threw up knickknacks, glass dogs, vases, fake flowers, and porcelain dolls over every square inch. Everything was covered in a thick blanket of dust.

Mr. O' Neil crossed his legs, exposing a hole in the toe of one of the threadbare slippers. He waved his hand in the direction of the coffee table like he really didn't care. I set the plate on the table and backed away, happy to be able to make my getaway.

"Just a minute, young lady," he snapped and pulled out a pair of glasses from a case on the end table. "What's your name again?" He slipped them on and stared at me, his eyes considerably magnified.

"Georgie," I said. "Georgie Tanner."

"Georgie? What kind of name is that? You named after your father? Your parents wanted a boy?"

I bristled a bit at that. I couldn't help it. I'd heard that question my whole life, and normally I was quite used to it. But his tone carried a mocking accusation that I just couldn't tolerate.

"Quite the opposite," I said. "I'm named after my paternal grandmother, Georgina Smith."

"Georgina, eh? Then *she* was named after her father." He said that with an emphatic nod. I opened my mouth to argue, when I realized he might be right. I needed to check a genealogy site to be sure, but I seemed to have earlier memories of a great grandfather named George.

"And your sons?" I asked. "Are either of them named after you?"

"Eh?" Immediately, a wary expression fell across his face. "What do you know about my sons?"

"From the pictures. On the wall." Apparently, this was not safe territory. I took another step toward the front door.

He scowled as he glanced at the hallway, where apparently he thought a portrait had betrayed his secrets.

"Doesn't matter now. Long ago," he grumbled.

My eyebrows lifted on their own at hearing him describe his children that way. Fortunately, Peanut decided to sniff around at my shoes. I squatted down to let the pup smell my fingers. When the white puff decided I was okay, I scratched the dog's ears.

"Cute dog," I said.

"What's that?"

"Peanut. She's a cute dog. Or is she a boy?"

"Meh." He shook his head. "She's a girl, and her name is Bear."

Bear? I stroked the hair back to see her brown eyes. "I thought you called her Peanut."

"Darn dog. Sissy name and that's all she answers to. Was my wife's doing." He trailed off, muttering. I saw this as my chance to escape. With one final pat on the dog's back, I stood to go.

"Okay. Well, I'll be seeing you. I'm sorry about our guest. If you ever find anything like that again on your property, please let us know. I'll take care of it right away."

There was no response. He had his arms crossed and seemed to be deep in thought. I cleared my throat. "I'll be seeing you later," I said, a little louder.

He made a shooing motion with his hand, still staring off into space. I did my best not to react to his actions, and instead walked back down the hall to the door. On my way, I passed the doorway to the kitchen. It was there that I could see what had made the loud banging noise. A kitchen chair that had fallen backward onto the floor.

I thought about righting it, but his voice rang out after me. "Go on. Get out of here."

What did Cecelia see in him? I couldn't get out of there fast enough, closing the door behind me.

CHAPTER 15

I drove to my apartment, ran up the stairs, and then locked the door behind me. From there I went straight to my bedroom and fell flat on my face on my bed. Some days I just did not want to be an adult. Give me a coloring book and some Pez candy. I'll let someone else make the decisions for a while.

I rolled onto my back and stared at the ceiling. Cobwebs had gathered in one of the corners. I needed to do some serious cleaning. It was weird how things I used to care about didn't matter as much anymore. I used to be a freak about cleaning. Every last inch of my home had to be wiped down. Now, it was more like five minutes as I ran through the house and then called it good enough.

Was it life that did that to me? Or death?

I thought about little Peanut. Or Bear. Whatever that tiny fluff's name was. She needed to get to the groomers. I wondered how long it had been.

Mr. O'Neil sure was crabby. I wondered if he'd found more cigarettes on his property before and that's what had him upset. I should have asked him if any had lipstick on the end.

Remembering the lipstick on the cigarette butt reminded me of the paper I'd found. I wiggled around until I could get my fingers into my pocket and pull it out. I flattened it on my knee.

The paper had a page number at the bottom—it was obviously from a book—and I reread the words to refresh my memory.

The butcher, the baker,

The candlestick maker

Turn them out, knaves all three.

A kid's poem. It seemed so odd and random. What book had this scrap been torn from, and why had it been clinging to the bush in our yard? Was it just a piece of random trash that had been blown in by the wind?

Or was it something important?

I studied the paper again. Another thing that made the scrap odd was that someone had doodled an ink drawing up the side. But whoever had torn it out hadn't thought the sketch was important, because the picture was ripped in half. I studied the drawing, trying to figure it out. Three swooping lines, and two triangles at the bottom.

I had no idea what it could be.

I'd have to think more about this later. Right now, I needed to take a shower. I placed the scrap in the top drawer as I got out clean clothes.

It was nearly an hour later when I finally came out. Once in the bathroom, I'd decided against the shower in favor of a bath. Thirty minutes of soaking with my kindle pepped me back up.

I was in the middle of towel drying my hair when my phone dinged. I wandered over to read it.

—GiGi! Where are you? Time for Dinner.

I chucked the phone on my bed and hurried to get ready. I'm going to be honest. One of my favorite things about moving back home was getting those home-cooked meals.

The bed and breakfast driveway was free of most of the cars, but Frank's was sitting in my usual spot. *Figures.* He'd better not give me a hard time about my interview earlier.

I walked in and immediately was hit with the scent of pot

roast. I seriously sighed out of gratitude when I saw the kitchen table.

Cecelia was old fashioned. There was freshly made bread and butter, mashed sweet potatoes, and green beans with bacon.

Of course, there was also Frank.

"Georgie," he said dryly.

"Frank," I shot back.

The kitchen counter was filled with dishes that had been washed and were now drying. I didn't know how Cecelia did it. Both she and Grandma could whip up a meal and wash the dishes as they went. It was a gene Grandma decidedly did not pass on to me.

"Glad you could make it," Cecelia said, before handing me a bowl of salad. She grabbed the salad dressing and we headed to the table.

"So, everyone ended up leaving, huh?" I asked her as I sat.

"We have the house to ourselves." She shook her napkin and smiled at us. "So nice to have a family dinner."

Spoons clattered against plates as we dished up and passed the serving platters.

"So, Frank," Cecelia started. "How are things going on the case?"

He breathed heavily. His lean face appeared haggard.

"What? It happens practically under my own roof and I can't ask?" Cecelia clicked her tongue.

"I just thought we could get through the sweet potatoes before you dove to the heart of the matter." He smiled and kind of caught me off guard. It'd been a while since I'd seen him smile.

"Well, honey. You know how I am. I like to know everything." Cecelia buttered a piece of bread. "And, since you're my favorite grandson, you should tell me."

"Coincidentally, I'm your only grandson, And yes, you do like to know everything, Grandma," he replied, the smile still there. I watched him shift and rub his chest. I couldn't help but frown. How could I have forgotten? He'd enlisted in the army immediately after high school. But his military career had ended when an IED exploded. He'd been in the military hospital for six weeks.

I watched as he uncorked the wine bottle.

"Want some?" he asked me as he carefully tipped the bottle over his glass.

I nodded, and he filled my glass a few inches, the red liquid swirling against the sides.

"Grandma?" he asked.

"No, thank you, Frank. And quit stalling."

"Honestly, I can't talk about that, Grandma." He forked in a mouthful of potatoes as if the food alone would save him.

"Oh, shush," Cecelia said with a wave of her hand. "Of course you can. It's just us."

"Just you and one of the witnesses, you mean," he said, now raising an eyebrow at me.

I shrugged. "It's just me. It's not like I'm going to tell anyone."

He sighed and rolled his eyes. Again, his hand went to that old scar on his chest.

"How about hypothetically?" Cecelia prodded.

"How about hypothetically, this could get me fired?" he shot back.

"Well, I have some news," I said.

They both turned to me.

"Who has the upstairs room on the right, overlooking the back yard?" I asked Cecelia.

She was shaking her head before I finished. "Why, no one, GiGi. Why?"

Hm. Well that put a damper on my clue. "Eliza Sue said she saw Mr. Peterson climb up the tree after a secret meeting with Rachel Green. Actually climb the tree! Her husband supposedly came out and nearly caught the two of them. I looked, and there isn't a screen on the window nearest to the tree."

Frank frowned as he took a sip of wine. "Rachel Green and David Peterson, huh?"

Cecelia zeroed in on him like a cat spotting a fly. "You've got something good. I can tell."

His eyes shifted away. "It's just curious, that's all."

"Franklin James Wagner! You better quit beating around the bush! Don't make me come after you with my slipper like I used to do when you were a little boy!" Cecelia scolded.

Frank set down the glass and glanced at his grandma. A twinkle sparkled in his eye, and his lips quirked like he might laugh. It was kind of funny to think of. This five-foot grandma shaking her finger at her much taller and bulkier grandson. But Frank acquiesced. "Well, Grandma, that threat's pretty scary." He turned to me. "This is not public info," he said, pointing his finger at my face.

I nodded, eager for any more information.

He scooped up a bite of meat and chewed thoughtfully. I could practically see the gears in his head turning: *do I tell or not?*

Finally, he spilled. "We found a connection between those two in Brooklyn."

"You're kidding me! What is it?" I asked.

"Peterson is a used car salesman. Apparently, the Greens spent some time looking at cars."

"The Greens were looking for a *used* car?"

"Apparently. Mr. Peterson and Mrs. Green spent quite a bit of time together trying to find the perfect one. Alone." His eyebrow arched at the last word.

"You think there might be some truth to them getting together, then. How did you find out?" I asked.

"This part I'm not too excited about. It was an anonymous tip."

"Why don't you like those?"

"Because I never know the motive of the person giving the tip."

I sat back, considering that. I may have thought Frank was a stick in the mud, but one thing I knew for sure. He was a darn good cop. I hated to admit it, but he'd impressed me a few times.

"Do you think Mr. Green knew?" I asked.

He scratched the back of his neck. "I'm not sure. Did you see anything that indicated they knew each other?"

I thought about it and shook my head, and then glanced at Cecelia. "How about you? You were here with them longer."

She pursed her lips and glanced at the ceiling. After a second, she answered, "No. As far as I knew, all seven of them were meeting for the first time. Although, there was one odd thing."

"Odd?" both Frank and I said at the same time.

I muttered, "Jinx, you owe me a soda," more from old habit rather than anything else. I was caught off guard when he grinned at me.

"Wow, does that take me back."

I smiled in return. "You probably owe me a thousand sodas. You never paid me back."

He shrugged. "What can I say? I was kind of a jerk."

I let that comment pass. It made me uncomfortable, and I

wasn't sure why. Quickly, I returned to the subject. "What was odd?"

"Well, Mr. Green said he'd been invited here. To our place."

"What?" I said. "Who invited him?"

"I'm not sure. He had the invitation and everything."

Frank leaned forward. "Are you serious? Where is it now?"

"Where is what? The invitation? Well, I hardly know. I suppose Mrs. Green took it with her when she left earlier."

Frank pulled out his phone and quickly texted. "We've got to track that down."

I was excited, too. It sounded like the first real clue.

Frank continued to text for a minute, and then put his phone away. He took another sip of his wine, deep in thought.

"Sheriff Parker told me you recovered a penny," I said. "A wheat penny that was used in the lamp."

He glanced at me like he'd forgotten I was there. "Oh. Yeah. It was still jammed in the socket. Not sure what to make of it yet. Those kinds of pennies aren't around a lot anymore. At the same time, it could have just been a coincidence. And we also know what the murder weapon was, a replica of a 1779 double-edged dagger, over nine inches in length."

My eyes widened.

"Well, it sounds like everything about that man was a quandary," Cecelia said. "More pot roast, anyone?"

"Did Mr. Green ever recognize you?" I asked Cecelia.

"Georgie!" she softly scolded. Her cheeks grew pink.

Frank narrowed his eyes at his grandma. "What's this? You knew him?"

Cecelia sighed. "I knew him years ago. When we were both in our twenties. I met him at his family's investing firm. We'd both just been hired on, so we bonded a little bit, being new."

"Bonded, huh?" He lifted a dark eyebrow.

She blushed and waved her napkin at him. "You stop now."

"You know, his investment firm's in some trouble," Frank said. "One of the local unions is going after them, saying they falsely invested the union's retirement fund. There's an audit going on, and Mr. Green's company is filing for bankruptcy as a result." He rubbed his jaw as his forehead furrowed with wrinkles. "This is definitely a puzzle. The guy has too many enemies, but none that fit the crime."

"Bankrupt! My goodness. And that business was so old." Cecelia sighed.

"You know," he said to me, "we're starting to lean in the

direction that someone was waiting in the building the entire time for you guys to show up. There was a break-in the night before."

I nodded. "I wondered if that was a possibility, but it seems so hard to believe."

"Well, there's one more suspect you both haven't thought of yet. You know how they say that building is haunted." Cecelia took a bite of her potatoes as if she hadn't said anything out of the ordinary.

"I think it's haunted all right, by something flesh and blood," Frank replied.

"As far as I'm concerned, it was only a matter of time before it happened." Cecelia shrugged.

"What do you mean, Cecelia?" I asked.

"That place has always been wrapped up in ghostly rumors. Maybe the soldiers have been waiting all this time."

CHAPTER 16

*A*fter helping out with the dishes and packaging the rest of the food to put away, I left Cecelia's for my apartment. I hurried to turn on the table lamp and wandered into my room. I chucked my purse on the dresser, and then eyed my bed. I was super tired.

Seconds passed as I stood there, staring at the bed. My body cried out with weariness. My brain felt numb. I hadn't tried to sleep on my own for a while. *It really might work tonight. I might be able to do it. I think I can.*

But the mere thought of attempting it made fear grip my heart, and I rushed into the kitchen. I couldn't face it. Couldn't face the nightmares that might show up.

I got a glass of water and scrambled for my sleeping pills. The

143

lid was stubborn and fueled the panic that was building inside me. Finally, it came off and a few pills spilled into my shaking hand.

Quickly, I swallowed one. I wandered to my bedroom feeling a combination of relief and guilt. It took about two nanoseconds after my head hit the pillow for me to fall asleep. Sleep I knew wouldn't be disturbed by the monsters in the dark.

The next morning, I woke up fairly refreshed. I walked into the kitchen. The prescription bottle stared accusingly at me as I poured a cup of coffee. Ignoring it, I took my mug and an apple into the other room. I had to get the right mindset on. Today might be another long day at Cecelia's, filled with squabbling guests.

I clicked on the TV and took a bite of my apple. I flipped through channels for a few minutes with no luck. Sometimes, I wondered why I even paid for cable. I was just about to give up when an English-accented voice stopped me. I paused for a second. The woman was cracking an egg and laughing.

"Now, do you know what to do when you crack an egg and get a shell in the batter?" She smiled into the camera.

I sat back and listened.

"Before you dig around to get it, wet your finger first. The shell will be much more likely to glom onto it." She did a quick demonstration.

I took another bite and watched her finish the recipe, homemade chocolate cake. It made me laugh at how easily entertained I was, but watching how she spun the cake on a glass pedestal while she frosted it was mesmerizing. She even covered it in scraped chocolate curls.

When it was over, I clicked off the TV, convinced I could make that.

Maybe.

After getting dressed, I threw back the last sip of coffee, chucked the apple core, and then headed out for the Baker Street B&B.

The house was quiet, with only Eliza Sue in the living room. Her curls were limp and she looked rather groggy, clutching a mug of coffee. I waved at her as I passed on my way to the kitchen.

"Good morning, GiGi," Cecelia said, her hands working with a pile of dough. She seemed to be moving a bit slower than usual.

"Good morning, Auntie. How'd you sleep?"

"Oh, I can't complain." She cut the dough in half and placed it into two greased pans. These she covered with a clean dish cloth and moved closer to the stovetop. "You got a phone call this morning."

"Here? Who was it?"

"Leslie Stilton from Three Maidens'. She asked if you could swing by the manor sometime today."

I got eggs and bacon from the fridge, wondering what the curator wanted now. "Can I have her number?"

Cecelia passed her phone over, and I dialed it up. Leslie answered on the third ring.

"Hi, Mrs. Stilton," I said and then remembered. "I mean, Leslie. It's Georgie Tanner. Cecelia said you wanted me to stop by?"

"Oh, hello! Would you have any time to do it today? Can we meet for lunch?"

"Sure, we can meet for lunch. Noon sound good? What's going on?"

"I just had some more stuff moved around." She hesitated. "Some very unexpected stuff."

My eyebrows went up. "Okay." I waited, but she didn't say anything more. "I guess I'll see you then."

I hung up the phone and started to tell Cecelia about the call.

Eliza Sue interrupted. "Excuse me. Can I get some more coffee?"

I nodded and got up to get the carafe. Then it was time to set the table. By the time everything was done, the rest of the guests were up and at the table. I'd have to talk to Cecelia later.

Breakfast ran late with everyone surprisingly relaxing at the table. Mr. Peterson said he had to go down to the station for a second interview, as did the St. Claires. There was more than a little bitterness in Mr. St. Claire's declaration. Mrs. St. Claire hushed him, saying it was his fault because he'd called the interview short yesterday.

Eliza Sue said she was going to pack up her belongings, with Sarah agreeing that she'd planned the same.

Satisfied everyone was going to be okay, I finished clearing the table. When I headed into the kitchen with my arms loaded with plates, I found Cecelia sitting at the table. Her eyes were closed, wincing, and she rubbed her temple.

"You okay?" I asked, setting the plates by the sink.

"Headache. One of my awful ones. I kind of wondered if it would happen when I woke up this morning. I had that funny feeling."

"Oh, no! Do you need your medicine?"

"I just took it. I'll be better in a little bit." She squinted at me. "Do me a favor, love, and run to the store for me? There's a few things I need right away. The list is by the coffee maker."

"Of course! I'll do it before I go see Leslie," I said. I hurried down the hall to the linen closet and snagged a washcloth. Quickly, I ran it under cold water and then handed it to her. "Take this for your head. Go rest. I've got this."

She accepted it gratefully and headed for her room. I washed the pans and loaded the dishwasher, and generally tidied up. I could hear the rest of the house growing quiet as the guests went about their day.

When everything was finished, I grabbed the list and headed out. It was a quarter to eleven. I was going to need to hurry to make it in time.

Outside, the only car still in the driveway was Sarah's. I headed for the van, hands in my pockets against the brisk air.

A blur of white streaking under the front tire caught my attention. I squatted down to look under the van. The little Pomeranian stared back at me. Well, like before, I assumed the pup was looking at me. Her fur still covered her eyes.

"Bear. Come here, Bear," I cajoled, making a soft snap with my fingers. The dog woofed. "What are you barking at? Come here, sweetheart."

The animal's tail wagged ferociously like a windsock in a storm, but the dog didn't budge. I tried a different tactic. "Peanut." A few kissy noises. "Come on, Peanut."

The dog scurried out from under my van, and into my waiting arms. Her tongue attacked my face.

"Sweetheart." I laughed, trying to duck. "What are you doing out here?"

I looked around but didn't see the neighbor anywhere. "Time to take you home." I carried the plump pup through the grass and then down Mr. O'Neil's driveway.

Nothing had changed from yesterday. The front porch still appeared old and decrepit. The piles of newspaper still lay in rotting piles. I shifted the dog in my arms and firmly knocked on the door.

"I'm coming. I'm coming," Mr. O'Neil yelled. "Hold your horses." He opened the door and stared at me through his glasses. He did not look impressed. "Oh. It's you."

I lifted my arms a bit to bring his attention to the squirming dog.

"Bear!" He gasped. "What in tarnation are you doing out here?" He reached for the dog, glancing at me again, this time with confusion.

"I found her running through Cecelia's property. Did she escape?"

"She darned well did. Must have squeezed through when I went out to get the mail. Don't you do that again, naughty girl," he murmured into the fur on her neck. "She probably thought she was going on a walk. Her momma used to do that for her."

His voice caught with pain. Silence drew out between us for a second or two. Then, he cleared his throat and scowled at me. "What do you want, a reward?"

Normally, his tone would have set me off. But I recognized it for what it was, a desperate defense because he'd been caught with the fracture to his heart wide open and unprotected.

"It's fine. I'm glad she's safe." I started to go and then hesitated. "You know, Mr. O'Neil, I wouldn't mind borrowing her from time to time. I like to walk, but not without a companion."

"You'd like that, would ya?" He pushed his glasses higher on the bridge of his nose and considered me. Finally, he nodded. "Well, we'll see. I'll let you know." He paused for a second. "And call me Oscar." With that, he shut the door.

I shook my head, wanting to chuckle. What a display of friendliness!

I glanced at the time on my phone and groaned. It was eleven. As I ran to the van, I put a call through to Leslie, to explain I had to run to the store, and that I might be a little late. After six rings with no answer, I hung up, hoping she'd understand.

I shoehorned my van into a parking spot at the back of the lot, and ran into the store with the grocery list. There were just a few things on the list, I should be in and out. The smell of pumpkin spice hit me from the coffee stand inside the store. I would have been tempted to get a drink myself, but several people stood in line already.

After a quick search, I had Cecelia's apples, lard, rhubarb, and brown sugar in the cart, and I was on my way to the checkout. Amy, one of my favorite checkers, was working, so I made my way into her line.

"Hey, lady!" she said by way of greeting and started to ring my things up. "I didn't know you baked."

I smiled as she weighed the apples. "This is for my aunt, but I might try my hand at it one of these days."

"Gotta keep busy, right?" She bagged the fruit. "Speaking of busy, how's the tour thing going?"

"Slowing down now that we're in autumn. But people are still visiting my website. I just got another one booked."

"I'm telling you, you need to add my grandpa's barn to your

tour. That thing has more history than half the places in town." She read the amount due. "That'll be seventeen fifty-two"

I handed her a twenty and she counted out the change.

"Two forty-eight," she said as she handed it back. She shut the register with a clang.

I stared at the change in my hand. One coin stood out from the rest.

A wheat penny.

"Something wrong?" she asked. She leaned forward and recounted it. "Yeah, two forty-eight, like I said."

I picked out the penny and held it up to her. "It's strange to see one of these, is all. Someone was just talking to me about them."

"Oh, a wheat penny. A customer came in last week and paid with a penny roll. The thing was almost filled exclusively with those."

"You're serious?" I could feel my eyebrows rise.

"Yeah. Pretty cool, huh? Probably why you never see them anymore. Someone's got them all collected."

"Do you remember who it was?"

Her gaze cut to the right as she tried to remember. "Hmm. I'll have to think about that. It was a busy day."

"Listen, could you call me if you remember?" I tucked the change back into my wallet and then smoothed out the receipt to give her my number. There was no pen around, except the fake one to write on the debit card screen. She saw me looking and pulled out a pen from her drawer. I scrawled out my number and handed it back to her.

"Are you a collector or something?" she asked as she read the number.

"Something like that. I'd really like to connect with the person." The bags were heavy as I picked them up.

"All right. If I remember anything, I'll give you a call. Have a good day." She smiled before turning to greet the person behind me.

I said goodbye, but she didn't see me. I was glad, because I'm sure I had a goofy look on my face, trying to puzzle out the penny.

I had a clue. I just knew it. But what kind was it? Had it been a customer simply paying with a penny roll and the murderer ended up with a wheat penny as change by coincidence? Or was it the murderer who was flaunting what he was about to do?

CHAPTER 17

I arrived at the Three Maidens' at about twenty past noon, having unloaded the baking supplies back at Cecelia's first. No one answered my knock at the door, but I thought I heard a voice answer back. The front door was unlocked, so I cautiously opened it.

"Leslie? You around?" I called and softly shut the door behind me.

No answer.

I took a step forward and nearly leaped out of my skin as the board under my foot gave off a sound like a gunshot. Darn it. I'd forgotten about that board.

"Leslie?"

Still no answer.

Okay. That's weird. I remembered she hadn't answered her phone when I'd called earlier. By now, I was sure that my frown lines were developing frown lines. The entryway seemed filled with dark shadows clinging to the corners. I could easily imagine some menacing ghost not at all happy that I was encroaching on its territory.

I didn't want to look for the curator, but I knew I had to. This could all just boil down to some simple explanation. I took a step forward, and another board squealed under my foot, not as loud as the first one, but unnerving nonetheless.

The urgency to be quiet—very, very quiet—held me in its icy grips.

On tiptoes now, I moved through the entry. I remembered tripping earlier on the candelabra on the floor and watched for it, but it was gone. I entered the hallway. It was almost completely dark, with all of the doors shut. I struggled to remember if it had been like this the last time I'd come through.

I pushed open the first door. Light dipped in from the windows of the old parlor. I was taken aback to see the furniture covered with black cloths.

Don't be silly. It's probably what she does after every tour to preserve things from the light and dust. Didn't she say she came here early to get things ready?

The curtains were pulled nearly closed but parted enough to see the dust motes dancing in a shaft of light. The room felt more haunted than ever.

Hair prickled on the back of my neck.

"Leslie?" This time I called at half-volume. My voice cracked in the middle. I swallowed and continued forward.

A squeak came from behind me, and I spun around to look. Nothing. Maybe just the floor settling behind me.

I passed the door to the basement. From what I remembered, the kitchen would be on my left. *Do I go downstairs?* My hand reached for the doorknob, but stopped short from turning it. A cold shiver ran through my body, and I knew I couldn't go down there. Not alone.

I silently eased into the kitchen, clutching my purse close to my body. I peeked in.

A teakettle was on the stove. Just as I caught sight of it, the kettle let out a squeal as the spout belched steam.

A scream flew up my throat, strangled when I realized what I was looking at. I saw two blue china mugs on the counter—obviously, she was expecting me—and felt instantly foolish.

She was around somewhere. Maybe she'd run to the bathroom.

Choking on nervous laughter, I called for her again. "Leslie?"

It was then that I spotted the shoe.

The tip of it peeked out from under a kitchen chair. I moved closer. It was just one, black with a rather low heel. The type a librarian might wear.

Or the curator of a haunted museum.

Quickly, I searched around for the other one as my mind scrambled for some way to explain the absurdity of one shoe. Perhaps she was after a spider? Maybe a bunion hurt?

No. No. No. My inner voice was very indignant at my musings.

The whistling of the teakettle was driving me nearly mad. I hurried over and moved the pot. I turned off the heat, noting it was a gas stove. The flames cut out with a *swick* sound. The teakettle's whistling slowly faded as if it didn't want to give up, but finally it went silent.

I didn't want to call for Leslie any more. A sick feeling was growing in my stomach. I shuffled my phone from my purse and held it, ready to dial 911. With my finger, I pushed open the door at the rear of the kitchen.

It opened to reveal a mudroom with a back door facing an overgrown garden.

It was getting darker in the house as the sky became overcast. The leaded glass windows let in a dingy gray gloom. As quietly as possible, I tip-toed back into the hall. I pushed opened the door to the bathroom, which was empty and surprisingly fitted with modern fixtures.

The final door led to a bedroom. A wire bed-frame stood in one corner, its thin mattress covered with an old, faded quilt. Clothing from that period hung behind glass on the walls, while an ivory brush with few remaining bristles sat on the wash stand.

No Leslie.

I glanced up the stairs to the second floor, but lost my nerve. My hands were shaking as I dialed Frank. It rang, two, three, four times, each ring tone sending my nerves rattling up the charts. *Answer! Answer! You're probably eating a doughnut. Where are you when I need you?*

"Frank here!" he said finally, right as I was about to hang up. I wanted to curse at how loud his voice came through the receiver, never mind his annoying greeting.

"Shhh," I hissed, glancing around the house. The shadows seemed to grow by the minute. "I'm at the Three Maidens' Manor. Where are you and how soon can you get here?"

"Who is this?" he asked suspiciously.

Really? Didn't he have caller ID? "It's Georgie," I gritted out. "You need to get here right away. Something's happened to Leslie."

"What's happened?"

I knew he was going to ask that. And no matter how I tried to convince him, he'd come back at me with a logical excuse of where Leslie was.

"Just come. Please. It's possibly an emergency."

"Why don't you call 911 then?" he asked, still deeply suspicious.

"Because I need you. Do it or I'll tell Cecelia what really happened to her silver spoons. Now come!" I hung up the phone, hoping my childish threat would motivate him to move.

He had a good point. Why didn't I call 911?

Because, in this town, every cop, paramedic, and reporter would show up. Half the town had scanners dialed in just waiting for something to pop up and break the monotony.

No, until I knew for sure, I needed to keep it quiet. Because it was possible that she was just outside in the garden, or down the road at the neighbors'.

159

Maybe she enjoyed wearing only one shoe.

But in my heart, I knew where she was and shivered.

I cast another look at the door leading to the basement stairs and flew out the front door.

CHAPTER 18

I paced in front of the old manor, skittish at every sound and falling leaf. The hammering of my heart didn't let up until I saw the police car turn down the old museum's driveway. Frank was inside, staring out the windshield with a sour expression.

He parked the car and climbed out. I thought he slammed the door unnecessarily hard.

"All right. What seems to be the problem?" He pulled off his hat as he walked toward me.

"It's Leslie. I was supposed to meet her here for lunch."

His gaze swept the front of the building. Sweat beaded on his upper lip. It was another warm autumn day, but not so warm as to explain the sweating. "And?"

"I can't find her anywhere. She's missing."

I thought he would give me a sarcastic answer, or at least an incredulous look. Instead, he studied the ground around the porch steps, his gaze moving back and forth. Slowly, he walked backward, scanning the driveway.

"What are you looking for?" I asked.

"A clue, if you haven't stomped all over it already." He hiked up his pants as he moved, still staring hard.

His pants seemed extra baggy. They weren't like that just a few weeks earlier. "You losing weight?" I asked.

"Let me work, would ya?" He squatted and pulled a pen out of his pocket. Carefully, he poked it at something on the ground.

Whatever it was, was concealed in a brown curled leaf. Frank flipped it over.

Small. White. Circular.

I walked over for a closer look. Frank pulled a plastic bag from his back pocket and tucked the object inside. He held the bag out to me for inspection.

It was a button.

"One in a million," he said. "Stood out to me because it's white."

"Anyone could have dropped that," I said.

"Anyone? How often do you just drop buttons? Usually they pop off, not fall off. But we'll see. Maybe it's nothing." He tucked the bag in his pocket. With a glance toward the house, he waved his hand. "Shall we proceed?"

I nodded. "I searched the ground floor. Didn't go upstairs or to the basement."

He raised an eyebrow. "The infamous basement."

A shiver rolled up my spine. "Yes, exactly that."

Frank keyed his shoulder mic and muttered a code into it. It squawked as someone returned with a message of "Copy that." He unsnapped his gun holster, and we started up the stairs.

"You think something weird is going on, too?" I asked.

"Between her not being here and the squealed-out tire tracks at the end of the driveway, let's just say I'm erring on the side of caution."

I looked over my shoulder to see if I could spy the tire tracks in the dirt. I didn't see anything out of the ordinary.

Frank had already ascended the porch steps and now stood in front of the door. I hurried after him.

He opened the door, and it made its usual long squeak.

"Leslie?" he called. He pulled out his flashlight and turned it on.

No answer. He walked inside. I huddled up behind him like his human shadow. "Leslie Stilton?" He missed the board that squealed, but I didn't, and we both flinched at the sound. Frank glanced at me with a look of disdain and a short jerk of his head to be quiet.

I shrugged slightly.

The two of us retraced my steps through the ground floor. Frank's gaze swept over each room. In the kitchen, he nudged the teakettle slightly on the stove with the butt of the flashlight.

I leaned forward to whisper, "I turned it off. It was boiling when I got here."

Frank's lips pressed together. We returned to the hallway and now stood before the basement stairs. Frank flexed his fingers a few times before opening the door.

Cold air curled out of the open doorway. We traveled down the steps, our shoes making hollow sounds on the treads. I remembered the filigree lamp that exploded in the hallway, and wondered if she'd replaced that.

Frank peered quickly around the corner, and drew back. "Police!" he yelled. "Leslie, you down here?"

My heart pounded. Leslie could be somewhere upstairs, oblivious to all this drama. Maybe she was asleep.

Frank flashed the beam of his Maglite down the hall. He cursed under his breath and ran to the end.

I followed him around the corner, trying to see what he'd seen.

The light was on in the room at the other end. The first thing I saw was a bare foot poking into the hallway.

Frank reached the room and checked quickly around the corner to be sure it was clear. He ducked toward the body. I came through the doorway just in time to see him take the woman's pulse on the floor. He swore again and yelled a new code into his mic. My jaw dropped at the sight of Leslie on the ground.

"Is she... is she okay?" I stuttered. This couldn't be happening. Not again.

Slowly, Frank turned her over. A purple knot stood out on her forehead like a plum. He felt again for the pulse. "It's there, but weak," he muttered. He tipped her head back to open her airway. "I don't know who did this to you, Leslie, but I'm going to find them."

The woman's eyelids fluttered. Her mouth moved.

Frank moved closer. "Say it again, honey. One more time."

Leslie moaned and then returned to shallow breathing. Frank didn't move.

I dropped to my knees next to the woman and squeezed her hand. "We're right here, Leslie."

The stimulation seemed to stir the woman again. Her eyes moved rapidly behind closed lids. She lifted her chin slightly.

Frank's mic squawked with an incoming code. He pushed the button to respond, "10-4." Then, leaning down, he spoke in a calm tone, "They're on their way, Leslie. Just hang tight. You're going to be okay."

Her lips parted again. I held my breath to listen.

Like a light breeze pulling the last leaf from a tree, Leslie whispered, "Revenge."

CHAPTER 19

I watched the EMTs shut the doors of the ambulance behind Leslie. My mouth was dry. Honestly, it was giving me a flashback. Taking me to another day, a little over a year ago, when I watched them take Derek away.

Derek.... The sight of the car swerving...the cliff. I still couldn't understand why he hadn't attempted to stop. I'd been following behind in my car....

I blinked my eyes hard. *Can't go there, not now.* My palms started to sweat, and I rubbed them on my pants.

Frank must have caught sight of my misery, because the next thing I knew he was standing beside me. He shifted his weight on his huge size twelve shoes—clodhoppers, as Cecelia always called them.

"How you doing?" he asked.

I chewed my thumbnail, not knowing how to respond. Was he referring to us finding Leslie just now, or...?

He rubbed the back of his neck and watched me. His eyes suddenly went soft and pitying, and he looked at the ground and cussed. Then his hand was on my shoulder, patting me like I was a prized pup. "You're going to be okay, Georgie."

It was then that I knew he was referring to Derek. His compassion almost did me in. I swallowed a lump in my throat the size of Everest and tried my best not to let the tears come. *Stop! No!* I gritted my teeth, but those hot tears came anyway. I turned away, feeling weak and sniveling.

Frank's hand dropped away. He sighed, and I wondered if he regretted even checking on me. With lumbering steps, he walked away.

I balled my hand into a fist and wiped my eyes. They say time heals all wounds. I'd like to find the person who first said that and wring their neck.

I frowned at my thoughts, my inner voice scolding me. *Kind of violent, aren't you, especially at a crime scene?*

I guess I was. I wanted to wring my inner voice's neck, too.

A paramedic climbed into the passenger seat of the ambulance after pounding on the door to assure those inside that it was locked. Another police officer, Jefferson, stood with Frank. They looked like they were going over their reports.

Frank pulled out the bag containing the button. More notes were taken, and then together, they walked to the end of the driveway. I presumed they were trying to find the tire tracks from earlier.

Weariness hit me like a ton of soggy pillows. I suddenly felt buried under emotion. I reached into my purse for the keys to the van, wondering if I could just follow the ambulance out, or if I needed to let Frank know.

Of course, the two officers had disappeared by then. The ambulance slowly pulled down the driveway, leaving me to stand in front of the museum alone. I glanced at it and shivered. Like a gaping mouth, the front door was left ajar. Years of safety conditioning made it difficult for me to leave with it open. But my nerves kept me from walking up there.

Frank and Jefferson were here, I reasoned. Getting home was probably the best thing mentally for me right now. People knew where to find me if they needed me.

I got into my van, pumped the gas, and it started with its usual coughs and sputters. Carefully, I backed down the driveway. At the end, I spotted the two officers examining tracks that curved to the right. Frank waved me down as I approached.

I slowed to a stop and rolled down my window.

He leaned in, bringing the scent of salty sweat and the cold outdoors with him. He rubbed his mouth with a leather-clad glove, not meeting my eyes. "You okay to drive?"

I nodded. "Yeah. I'm fine."

His eyes met mine briefly, as if to check for himself. "I'll see you tonight, maybe." With that, he leaned back and banged the door with the flat of his palm. "Drive safely."

I left him wandering back to the tire tracks. I can't say I went straight home. I should have, I knew it. But my mind was a wreck, filled with unbidden memories. Before I could get back to my real life and "fake it," I knew I had to pack those memories away.

The best way I'd found to do it was a long drive. I'd taken a few over the last year. Memory drives, I called them. I'd drive and drive, and sometimes be surprised at where I ended up. It was a little scary to realize I'd zoned out and was not able to recall exiting off the highway, or taking that turn up a mountain road. But suddenly, as if waking up from a dream, I'd look around and realize I'd gone as far as I'd wanted. That's how I'd know the memories were packed away. I'd pull over and program my GPS for home, feeling sane again.

This time was no exception. By the time I took a good look around me, I was in the Pocono Mountains, nearly two hours from home. *Wow, I really did it to myself this time,* I thought, as I typed in my home address.

My drive home was filled with thoughts of Leslie. Who had hurt her? Why had she muttered the word revenge? Did it have something to do with the ghosts that supposedly haunted the building?

I flipped my blinker and merged back onto the highway. Ghosts weren't known for leaving behind buttons, if Frank's clue was to be believed.

This had to be about Mr. Green's murder. Whoever it was must have returned to the scene of the crime because they'd left something behind. Something that could incriminate them.

Leslie hadn't said anything else after her last words, succumbing completely to unconsciousness from the blow to her head. Whoever it was mustn't have known I was coming. I shivered. Was he or she still at the manor when I arrived?

And then there were the tire tracks. Were they really connected? If so, what had made the perpetrator leave so quickly? Was it one of the guests of the bed and breakfast? Would I be eating dinner tonight with the person that had hurt Leslie?

CHAPTER 20

*A*fter my long drive, I went straight to my apartment. I wasn't ready to head back to the bed and breakfast. I didn't want to see anyone, didn't want to have to put my customer service face on and smile. It was a great relief when I shut my door.

I was alone. I quickly went to the desk and pulled out a spiral pad of paper, along with a pen, and took them to the bed. If I wanted to figure out who hurt Leslie, I needed to figure out who killed Mr. Green.

Okay, what do I know? I clicked the end of the pen and started a list.

A button.

A strange scrap of paper with a poem.

The possibility that Mr. Peterson knew Mr. St. Claire in Brooklyn.

The conversation Mr. Peterson overheard between the St. Claires.

The possibility that Mrs. Green was pregnant and it wasn't her husband's.

The night rendezvous Eliza Sue spoke of between Rachel and Mr. Peterson.

How Mr. Peterson had offered to accompany Rachel to the hospital.

The tampered lamp and the penny.

The fact that Cecelia knew Mr. Green from years ago and worked with him.

The fact he was killed with a replica 1779 dagger.

The possibility that Mr. Green's company committed fraud with a local union's pensions, and because of the investigation, his company was now filing for bankruptcy.

The questionable tire tracks left at the museum.

I chewed on the end of my pen before reminding myself of my front tooth crown. The crown stemmed from a broken tooth I'd gotten as a teenager, trying to use a speed bump to jump the railroad tracks a week after I got my driver's license.

Frank had shaken his head at me like I was stupid, before sneaking me out the next night to jump the tracks in his new car.

I smiled at the memory.

The light in my room darkened. I glanced out the window to see clouds blowing in to cover the sun. A black line on the horizon warned of an approaching storm.

I shivered. Amazing how quickly the temperature dropped with the sun blocked. The winds had picked up too, snatching the last leaves from the trees and cartwheeling them through the air. Okay, enough alone time. I needed to get back to the bed and breakfast and help out with dinner.

I DROVE up to Cecelia's. Frank's police car was already there, parked in the narrow space between the house and the storage shed to one side. I turned off the engine and Old Bella gave her usual shudders and jerks.

The wind felt like it had teeth as it bit through my coat. I guessed winter was here to stay now. Mr. Peterson was standing on the front porch smoking a cigarette. He had his jacket bundled up to his neck and was hunched inside.

"You cold?" I asked.

Smoke swirled around his head as he nodded. He sniffed and wiped his nose with the back of his hand.

"Everyone's inside, if you're curious," he said.

I figured as much. Not a lot to do in this small town once everything closed down for the night.

"Dinner ready?" I asked, by way of small talk. I knew it was about time. I could smell the ham from where I was standing.

He shrugged, and I headed across the old porch. The screen door squeaked its normal welcome, and I walked inside.

I was greeted with women yelling from the back bedroom.

Not. Again.

"Give me that!" one yelled.

"Don't you touch it!" said another.

I inwardly groaned and hurried down the hall to the room.

"Oh, hello," Sarah said, catching sight of me as I peeked in. Her hair was in its customary messy bun, which was even more messy than usual, now sliding sideways down her head.

"What the heck's going on in here?" I asked, leaning against the door frame with my arms crossed.

Sarah held a book in her hands that she glanced down at guiltily. She held it out toward me as if for my approval.

Eliza Sue was shooting daggers with her eyes at Sarah. "You have no right."

"What is it?" I asked, accepting the book. Seeing it in my hands, Eliza Sue simmered down.

The book was tiny, palm size, the cover held shut with a piece of string. I turned it over in my hands. The title said, "Christmas book compilation." It felt very old.

Eliza Sue crossed her arm. "I came around the corner and saw Sarah in here. Snooping around."

Sarah let out a screech. "That's not true! You were!"

Eliza Sue yelled back. The accusations started flying back and forth faster than I could understand, and it was escalating quickly.

"All right! Cool it!" I yelled.

"You say Sarah was snooping. Well, what were you doing in here?" Mr. Peterson asked. I turned, startled to see him behind me. I hadn't heard him enter.

"How dare you!" Eliza Sue was positively shaking. "Let's talk about your private time with Rachel. Disgusting cheater!"

Mr. Peterson's nostrils flared. "That's a lie!" he yelled. His gaze switched between Sarah and me. "I already told you she's lying."

"I saw you that night," Eliza Sue said. "Remember? But what can we expect from someone of your calibre with your 'high' used-car dealership work ethics?"

His fists clenched. I honestly thought he might strike her.

"All right!" I yelled. "That's enough. You. Leave now." Even though he was so much taller than me, I grabbed Mr. Peterson by the elbow and steered him out the door. And then to the women. I said, "I'll take the book. Did the Greens leave anything else?"

Eliza Sue shook her head. "I don't know."

"Fine. You two head out. I'll search this room, and then contact Mrs. Green."

"You're going to mail it?" Eliza Sue asked.

"Most likely. After I take inventory. That's the bed and breakfast's policy."

She nodded stiffly. "Good."

The women left.

I listened a minute to check if there was any more yelling. It was with great relief when everything stayed silent. Quickly, I checked under the bed and found a pair of shoes. I set them by the door, wondering what Sarah was even doing in here. I yanked open the dresser drawer, but it was empty. There was a brush between the nightstand and the bed.

Stuff in hand, I walked into the kitchen.

Cecelia was a welcome sight after this long day. She was stirring liquid cornstarch into some of the ham's drippings that she'd already pulled off to make gravy. Cecelia's gravy could not be beat.

"Hi, Auntie," Still clutching the items, I walked over to give her a hug. "How's the headache? You find all your groceries okay?"

"Hi, you!" she said cheerfully, still whisking like a madman. She offered the side of her head on my shoulder as a quick hug back. "I'm fine. Everything's fine. But I haven't seen you all day, so I've been worried."

"Oh. You heard about Leslie?"

"Heard? Of course I heard! Even Joel down at the post office heard. He called me right away to make sure you were okay."

"Aw, that's sweet. It's always something around here. I need to call the hospital to check on the poor woman. Hey, do we have any extra boxes? The Greens left some stuff behind."

"Check in the pantry for a shipping box."

I walked in. Sure enough, there were several on the floor of all different sizes. I deposited everything but the book into one and set the box on the kitchen table. A basket sat there, too. It was Cecelia's sewing basket. I recognized it from the years of being a rough kid and always ripping my shirt or jacket. Of course, the overalls had been indestructible.

"What's the sewing basket out for?" I asked her.

"Oh, Eliza Sue said Mr. Peterson asked her to fix something for him. His shirt tore or something."

Obviously, that was way before this big fight. I doubt they'd be talking to each other again anytime soon. "I saw Frank's car. Is he here?"

She set the gravy to one side. "Oh, he's out in the back someplace. Wind blew down a few branches. I should text him to let him know dinner is ready."

Her phone was on the table. I smiled as she sent off a text. It still felt funny seeing this white-haired lady be so tech savvy and reliant. She washed her hands and pulled a casserole dish from the oven. Then she slipped dinner rolls in to warm.

"Did you find a box? What sort of stuff did they leave? Anything that requires special packing?" she asked.

I paused, studying the book one more time, before walking over to show her. "This book is pretty valuable, I guess."

She glanced at it as she wiped her hands on the kitchen towel.

"Really! That looks quite old. It almost looks like an heirloom. What an odd thing to bring on a vacation."

It was an odd thing. It made me even more curious about what was written inside. I lifted an eyebrow in an unasked question.

She laughed at my expression. "Well, I want to know what it says, too."

The back door crashed open, and Frank came through, stomping his feet to rid himself of any leaves. He caught sight of me and nodded a welcome. "Starting to rain," he said to his grandma.

He walked over to the sink to wash his hands.

I leaned against the counter next to him.

"What do you want?" he asked, his voice gruff.

"Oh, nothing," I said, lifting the book to his eye level. "Just discovered something in Mr. Green's room. I'm sure it's quite boring, really."

Frank's gaze flicked to the book and then back to me. He brusquely turned off the water and stomped over to get the towel to wipe his hands.

Cecelia was just pulling out the rolls when he nearly bumped into her. She shooed him. "You're right under my feet. You two go set that table."

He walked back to me, tongue in the corner of his cheek. "Found it, huh?"

I nodded, waving the book in front of his face like a hypnotist's sparkly watch. "Yep. Wonder what's inside?"

The corner of his lips quivered. Just the corner, but it was the beginning of a smile and I knew I had him. He reached a hand out. "Let me see it."

Of course, I was happy to hand it over. Police business and all that. I hovered at his shoulder as he slowly unwound the cord.

"The table, Frank!" Cecelia yelled.

"One second, Grandma!" He had the cord unwound. I held my breath as he cracked the cover.

My heart did a double beat, I swear it did, when I saw those pages.

Yellow. Soft.

Just like the piece I'd found earlier.

CHAPTER 21

I must have made a noise then, because Frank's eyes cut sideways at me.

"I think if you flip through it, you'll notice there's half a page missing somewhere," I said, swallowing my excitement and trying to appear calm.

He didn't answer, but gently flipped the pages to check. The old paper made a soft swish as he rifled through.

He paused halfway and carefully opened the book more. I leaned in, chewing my bottom lip.

There it was. The page was torn. And what was left was the remains of the drawing and what looked like a poem.

He read it out loud.

Rub a dub dub,

Three fools in a tub,

And who do you think they be?

We both looked at each other when he finished.

"That's a kids' poem," I said.

"I know what it is," he said dryly. "Go get your missing piece."

"In a minute. What's it say at the beginning of the book. Any dedication?"

"I'll 'in the minute' you two!" Cecelia scolded, her cheeks pink. She grabbed the dining service basket. "I'll just do it myself, thank you."

"Sorry, Grandma," Frank said, not looking the least bit sorry. He flipped to the front of the book.

The Christmas Box

A collection of stories and songs by James Halliwell-Phillipps

The date below said 1830.

"Wow," I said as Frank simultaneously whistled. "You think this is really that old? Or a reproduction?"

"There *is* a dedication here," he murmured, after flipping

another page. We nearly butted heads leaning down to read it.

"Darling Samantha. May you know where I hid it. Go for it when it's safe. Your loving mother, Elizabeth Hartwell."

"Treasure?" I whispered. "Is that what she's referring to?"

Frank actually rolled his eyes. "Girl, you still think you're nine and we're playing pirates. No, this isn't about treasure."

"What? How can you know that?"

"It says, 'where I hid it.' We don't know what *it* is."

"And you are acting like an unimaginative stick in the mud, just like you did that one winter when your grandma told you that Jack Frost was the one who put the designs on the windows. You demanded to know who he was, including some proof."

"Well, I knew he was made up."

"We all did. We were having fun."

"Really. Are you pretending now?" His eyebrow rose in that "gotcha" kind of way.

Darn it, he did have me. Once again, I'd managed to give him the only kind of argument he could use against me. It was a scenario I'd often repeated through the years with him.

"Go get your paper," he said.

"I can't. It's at my apartment," I replied.

"Dinner!" Cecelia called. "Come and get it."

"You know what you're getting for dessert," he grumbled, sliding the book into his inside jacket pocket. "A big serving of 'a cold car ride through a rainy night.'"

I sent him a stiff smile and grabbed the two pitchers of ice water on the counter. Without another look in his direction, I sauntered into the dining room, head held high. I couldn't believe how quickly Frank had me squabbling with him, just like when we were kids. He was beyond annoying.

But I needed his help to figure this out.

I slowly filled the water glasses while the other house guests filed through the door. I was a little worried at how Mr. Peterson and Eliza Sue would interact, but it seemed like, for now, they'd called a truce.

Cecelia had done an amazing job decorating the table. The room glowed under the flicker of red candles at the table's center. Surrounding them were silk leaves, pine cones, and baby pumpkins. Red linen napkins, heavy silverware, and white china plates completed the effect.

Cecelia continued to bring out food in white tureens and platters. Ham, scalloped potatoes, marshmallow-topped sweet potatoes, baskets of rolls, butter and homemade raspberry jam, salad and dressing, along with gravy, lined the center.

As I sat, I glanced around the table, happy to see faces relaxing, and even soft laughter break out among the guests as the food was passed around.

I was torn between taking my time and enjoying the amazing meal, and hurrying back to my apartment for the scrap of paper. I took a bite of ham and sighed. The food definitely deserved the time to appreciate it.

My eye caught Frank's, and he made a hurry up motion with his fork. Just for that, I grabbed a roll and slowly buttered it before asking that someone pass the jam.

His eyes rolled toward the ceiling, and he sighed while I bit into it.

"So," I started, "What's everyone been up to today?"

"Not much," Mr. Peterson answered. "Another day, another interview. Just hanging around town waiting for the good ol' sheriff to say we're free."

Frank narrowed his eyes but didn't say anything.

"Mmm, this is so good," Mrs. St. Claire said after a bite of sweet potatoes. "What do you think, Jared? Don't you love it?"

Her husband nodded next to her, his mouth full.

"You know what this reminds me of?" Her voice carried over the rest of the conversations. "This reminds me of when Jared and I first met." She smiled in anticipation of her story. "I was doing a food run for the local Girl Scouts. They were having their troop meeting at my house. Anyway, there I was looking for marshmallows..."

"When you pinched my stuff," Mr. St. Claire said with a wry grin. His eyes twinkled behind his glasses.

Mrs. St. Claire laughed. "I didn't pinch your stuff! What happened was we were in the same aisle. I got my marshmallows and threw them in the cart. I turned to look at something, before heading to the next aisle to search for the graham crackers."

"That's when she pinched my cart."

Mrs. St. Claire shook her head. "I didn't realize. You let me get away." She swatted her husband's arm in playful jest.

"I was admiring the view." His eyebrow curled up, along with the corner of his mouth.

She blinked coquettishly, her red-lipsticked lips drawing back into a huge grin.

I studied Mrs. St. Claire, chewing slowly. I remembered her telling me just the other day how she'd met her husband.

She'd said she met him in Florida on the beach. She and her husband seemed so innocuous, just a couple in their early forties out for their anniversary. Why would she lie about something like that? And what else had she told me that wasn't true?

CHAPTER 22

After dinner and farewells, Frank followed me in his police car to my apartment. Even in this small town, it was always a little difficult finding parking. I finally edged the van into a space about half a block from where I lived.

It was still sprinkling outside. Of course it was. I grabbed my jacket from the passenger seat and climbed out. Quickly, I shrugged into it and pulled up the hood, buttoning it as I hurried along the sidewalk.

Frank was waiting for me at the entrance to the building. I punched in the passcode and the door unlocked. He yanked open the door and stepped back, allowing me to enter first. By the time we finally reached the fourth-floor landing after climbing dozens of stairs, Frank was puffing a bit.

"You okay?" I asked, reaching into my purse for my house key.

"Yeah," he said, before coughing into his fist.

"You've seemed kind of off today." I led him to my door and unlocked it. I'd forgotten to leave a light on again. I stumbled across the room for the lamp while Frank waited by the door.

"There!" I said as I flipped the switch. I glanced around the room, a little afraid I'd left the place in a total disaster, but it was okay. I kicked some socks under the coffee table and scooped up a few dishes and carried them to the sink.

His hands were in his pockets. He watched me with the slightest smile. "Well?"

"Oh, yeah." I hurried into my room where I'd left the book scrap on my desk. Fragment in hand, I walked back to the living room.

Frank was studying a painting on the wall. One I'd done just a few months ago. It was of a creek where we used to play as kids. A place that meant summertime and fun. Safety. Happiness. I stopped, overcome with a weird sense of exposure and shyness.

He looked in my direction. "This is good," he said. "Is that really your name in the corner?"

Heat filled my cheeks. I tried to distract him, hoping he

wouldn't recognize the place. "Yep. Hey, I've got the paper. Come into the kitchen and I'll make you some tea. Or something stronger."

He ignored me and turned back to the painting. The flush in my face was crawling down into my shoulders, and I stared at the ground. I'd never shared my work before, and to have *him* of all people studying it, well, I wished a hole would open up in the floor.

He didn't say anything, and after a moment, I dared to glance up at him. His eyes were contemplative. I was wondering if he was remembering a simpler time, too. His jaw moved like he was biting the inside of his cheek. Finally, he heaved a sigh and turned back to me.

"Yeah. Good." His words seem to carry a tone of respect. Then he was back to business. "Now, let's see the paper."

I passed it over to him. Frank took it as he dug in his pocket for the book. He walked over to the couch and sat, leaning forward with the book on the coffee table. Carefully, he flipped to the torn page and then unfolded the scrap I'd found.

I could already see by the color of the paper that it would be a match. He slid it into place.

He read the finished poem.

Rub a dub dub,

Three fools in a tub,

And who do you think they be?

The butcher, the baker,

The candlestick maker.

Turn them out, knaves all three.

Now the poem was complete and so was the sketch. It turned out that the part I had was the bottom flowing lines of a dress. The top part that had been left in the book was her face. Her hand pointed to the first line of the poem.

The sketch was not original to the book. It must have been penned at some later date. It was so unusual, I couldn't stop staring.

"Odd. Very, very odd," Frank mumbled.

"I agree." I took the book from him and carefully flipped through the rest of the pages. When I reached the back, something fell out to the floor.

I reached down to pick it up, my jaw dropping as I realized what it was. "Frank! It's the invitation! The special one Mr. Green said he got to come to the bed and breakfast!"

Frank leaned over to read it. It was decorated with hearts and kisses. I turned it over.

He snorted. "This was just a sexy invite from his wife. 'Let's hang out at the Baker Street Bed and Breakfast and Make History.' With a kiss mark? It's obviously from Rachel. He probably told Grandma that he got a 'special invitation' tongue in cheek."

I was incredibly disappointed. What he said made sense.

"So, what are you going to do with the book?" Frank asked.

"I'm supposed to take inventory of everything the Greens left and box it all up. I guess we'll mail it next week."

"What else did he leave?" He leaned back on the couch, his arm resting across the top.

I ran through the list of the shoes, brush, and other odds and ends. Nothing stood out as important. "I just don't understand why the page was torn out."

"You and me both, girl." Frank sighed. He snapped a picture of the torn page and shut the book. "I'm half tempted to take this in as evidence, but I can't see a correlation yet."

"Well, if I come up with anything, I'll let you know," I answered. Neither of us said anything more. The silence grew. Suddenly, it felt awkward. I cleared my throat just as he coughed.

"All right. I guess I'll see you later. Tomorrow maybe," he said, rising from the couch.

"Yeah. Anything special happening tomorrow?"

"As far as I know, the chief is going to release the guests. Everyone will be free to go home."

"No more leads?" I was worried.

"We're still investigating, but I think he feels we have all we need from them right now."

"What do you think?"

He shook his head. "I think I'm going to hunt a murderer. And I'm going to catch him."

His eyes had a steely glint to them that made me shiver. I nodded. His boots thumped as he walked to the front door.

"Okay then. I'll see you tomorrow, then maybe," I said.

With a nod at me, he shut the door behind him.

I went to the cupboard for a mug and started making myself some of that tea I'd offered Frank earlier. My mind mulled over that piece of paper.

What were some reasons that I'd tear out a piece of paper? I thought about it as I put the mug in the microwave and opened a chamomile packet.

I did it for grocery lists.

And for addresses.

The microwave beeped, making me jump. I lifted out the mug and steeped the teabag.

An idea was growing in my mind. I grabbed my phone and carried my tea to the couch. It was cold in the apartment, so I curled up in one corner and pulled the throw blanket off the back to cuddle into. After wrapping it around my knees, I turned to the torn page of the book. Carefully, I typed the poem into the search bar. A link came up and I clicked it.

What?

My mouth dropped open. I read it again. Excited, I jumped forward, nearly upsetting my mug. As quickly as I could, I called Frank.

He answered on the first ring.

"Frank! Hurry and get back here! Your hunch was right. You have to take this book into evidence. You're not going to believe what it means!"

CHAPTER 23

$\mathcal{I}$ gave him the code to the building, and ten minutes later, he was pounding on my door. I opened it with the biggest grin. I could barely contain my excitement.

Frank was not so excited, and stopped to inspect the door. "This thing almost opened just by me knocking." He scowled at me. "A good-looking girl like you...." He spun back around as if he were still examining the lock. I could see the back of his neck redden. He was finally caught off guard by something stupid he'd said. Point for me.

"Come on. Look what I found!" I called as I headed for the couch.

Frank followed me. I clicked on the article and passed the phone over to him.

He squinted at the screen and held the phone away, trying to focus.

"Well?" I said.

He read it out loud.

"The original lyrics to Rub a dub dub.

Hey! rub-a-dub, ho! rub-a-dub, three maids in a tub,

And who do you think were there?

The butcher, the baker, the candlestick-maker,

And all of them gone to the fair."

He set the phone down. "And that's exciting because...?"

I couldn't believe he didn't get it. "Don't you see? The scrap of paper. It was an address. Three Maidens' Manor. Elizabeth Hartwell was directing her daughter to the house."

"How on earth could you have guessed that out of all the places in the world, she meant this one here in Gainesville?"

"Well, I never would have *if* the book wasn't here in this town, and *if* that scrap hadn't been torn out. It made me think

CHERRY PIE OR DIE

of times I'd torn off a piece of paper. The woman in the sketch is pointing to the first line, which made me think it was pretty important. So I searched it up, and that's the line that stuck out to me. Something is hidden in that house."

"Problem one, it's the second part of the poem that's torn off, not the first part referring to the maids. And what do you think this has to do with Mr. Green's murder?" he asked, settling back into the couch. He propped his mud-crusted boots on the coffee table and looked at me.

"Err." I leaned over and pushed his feet to the floor. "So far, I've only spent about two seconds on research. I don't know why the second part of the poem was torn out, and not the first. But the book looks like an heirloom and was in Mr. Green's room. I searched Elizabeth Hartwell's name. Turns out both she and Samantha are related by however many great-grandmas to Michael Green."

"Really?" he asked. He looked slightly impressed.

I shrugged. "Took all of a minute on that genealogy site."

His eyebrows rose and he nodded. "So it's safe to assume Mr. Green wasn't here by accident. He was here looking for something."

"But remember the invitation," I added. "Was he looking, or was someone looking for him?"

"That definitely makes the invitation more interesting. Whoever it was, they found him, all right. Question is, was it one of Grandma's guests? Or was there someone else at Three Maidens' waiting?"

I grabbed my tea and took a sip, contemplating. "I wonder if this takes Rachel off the suspect list."

"You mean for life insurance reasons as her motive?" he asked.

"No. Well, maybe. I was thinking more about her possible pregnancy that wasn't her husband's."

Frank sat straight up. "Wait. What? When were you going to let me in on that little nugget?"

I bit my lip and set the mug on the table. "Oh, sorry. It's just a rumor that the other guests have been gossiping about. I don't even know if it's really true."

He narrowed his eyes at me.

Change the subject. "You know, I just remembered Leslie talking about someone who broke into the museum the night before. Well, guess what? Mr. Peterson was outside that night. A couple of people saw him." I bit my thumb nail. "I have a bad feeling about him. Maybe it was him that broke in? When he first showed up, he told me he was a history buff. And, I forgot about this, but Eliza Sue had to fix his shirt today. He tore it or something. You think he could have lost the button?"

He closed his eyes as his head flopped back. "You're kidding me. Why do you not go to the police about this stuff?"

"What? I'm supposed to report everything I think is weird? I'd be there every ten minutes. Besides, it's probably nothing. Who would I even tell?"

He thumbed the badge on his shirt and lifted an eyebrow. "They're called police officers. Call the station and try it sometime."

"Well, I'm telling you now."

Frank had that smart-aleck smirk on his face that made me want to scream.

"He's already on your radar, isn't he? You said you found a link between Peterson and Rachel back in Brooklyn."

"Yeah, our anonymous tip." He exhaled loudly and stood, scooping up the book. "You have anything else to share?"

I shook my head.

"Call me with anything else you find out." He gave me a serious stare.

I was tempted to enter a stare down. Instead, I opted to act casual, fluffing the blanket around my legs and reaching for my mug again. "Of course. Anything that seems serious, I'll let you know."

"Anything you hear," he reiterated.

"Absolutely. Anything of importance."

"You are infuriating, woman," he growled.

I took another sip, staring at him over the mug's rim.

He shook his head, exasperated, and stalked to the door. At the doorway, he announced, "Anything you find!" before slamming it behind him.

I smiled and snuggled deeper into the cushions. He may have knocked me off guard about the painting, but I'd definitely won round two.

CHAPTER 24

I woke up the next morning after another dreamless night. I'd really intended to go without the sleeping pill, but at the last minute, I chickened out again.

"I'll deal with it. I really will," I told myself in the mirror. The last few weeks made me think I needed to get back to seeing a therapist again. Maybe I was ready to move on.

But I'd do it on my own terms. Not in some middle of the night paralyzing nightmare.

Cecelia had texted me to say it was going to be a continental breakfast, and I needn't hurry down. Today, my plan was to help everyone pack and say goodbye, and then head to the hospital to check on Leslie. They wouldn't give me any news over the phone, so I thought I'd try and go see for myself.

Honestly, though, it was kind of disappointing and anticlimatic that the guests were leaving. I couldn't believe the police hadn't figured it out.

Mr. Peterson came to mind. I hoped I wouldn't shiver when I said goodbye to him. And to think of him and Rachel.... I just didn't know what to believe.

I had to park Old Bella near the end of the B&B's driveway, it was so filled with cars. As I walked up to the door, I heard the sound of clippers.

I peered down the property line. "Hey, Oscar! How are you doing today?"

He looked up, clippers in hand. His eyebrows lowered over his eyes. "How am I doing? Got the gout, the start of shingles across my butt, and I need some Imodium. Is that what you wanted to hear?"

The little Pomeranian saw me and barked to catch my attention. "Hi, Bear. How are you, sweetheart?" The dog wagged her tail so hard her whole body wiggled. Her pink tongue hung from her panting mouth. She ran to the base of the bushes and squirmed through. I met her on the other side crouched on my heels. She nearly bowled me over in her enthusiastic ferocity to lick my cheek. Laughing, I steadied her on two legs so that she could give me a kiss.

"Well, even my dog's betrayed me, I guess," Oscar grumped. He snipped back a few more branches.

I gave her a kiss on her fuzzy-topped head, and then pushed the branches apart so she could scoot back through.

"I don't know about that," I said with a smile.

"Yeah, well, let's see who she prefers after you walk her a time or two." His brows rose. "You have time today? You probably don't have any time today. You young people always say one thing and—"

"Tomorrow afternoon would work perfectly," I said. "I'll be completely free."

He harrumphed and continued to prune. But I thought he looked pleased.

"All right, well, I need to head inside and help these guests get out of here. I'll see you later."

"Well, we'll see about that. And bring over another piece of pie!"

I grinned as I walked up the porch. Mr. Peterson was coming out as I entered, tapping his cigarette pack.

"Last day, and you're getting rid of us. Are you going to have a party after we leave?"

"Absolutely not. You've all been wonderful," I answered, my customer service smile at a hundred watts.

He snorted. "Yeah. I bet you think that." He reached into his pocket for his lighter.

I studied his shirt. I couldn't help it. My eyes went to his buttons.

He glanced down. "What? I got a stain on me or something?"

I shook my head. "No, no. Sorry. Just spacing out for a second." I smiled again, and went inside.

The living room was empty for the first time since everyone had arrived. I wandered upstairs to check on the guests.

Two doors were open upstairs. I peeked into the first and saw Eliza Sue. She was reading a book, her suitcase already packed and waiting by the door. She looked like a librarian, sitting there in her dark blue cardigan and matching shoes.

"How are you doing?" I asked.

She glanced up before sliding a bookmark into the pages. "I'm good. Tired. Ready to go home."

"Mind if I come in?" I entered when she waved me in. "Now, where's home again?"

"Brooklyn. I work at an accounting company down there."

CHERRY PIE OR DIE

"What are you reading?"

"*The Time Before Dawn*. It's a non-fiction piece on the Dark Ages." She held up her book so I could read the title. "I love history. You know what they say, those who don't learn history are doomed to repeat it."

"That's so true. You know, there was a time, years ago, when I considered being a history teacher."

"Really? Why didn't you do it?" she asked.

"Honestly? I think you need a special temperament to work with kids. I ended up becoming a paralegal for an estate lawyer and that was a much better fit. But, teachers are pretty amazing."

She nodded. "They really are. Teaching is about sacrifice. You have to have quite the integrity to do it."

"I agree. Do you need any help with anything?"

Eliza Sue shook her head. "No. I'm just waiting for Sheriff Parker to let us go."

"I expect it's going to be sometime soon. Sorry your second vacation was like this. I hope you book something else soon for yourself."

"Don't be sorry for me. I'm fine. But poor Mr. Green. Did you get his stuff packed up?"

"Yes. It's at my apartment. I'll wait a couple of days to ship it, just to make sure we didn't miss anything else." I fudged a little on the whereabouts of the book. I didn't want to let anyone know that the police had taken it into evidence.

"Good plan." She nodded, her dark curls bobbing. "I've always double-triple checked hotel rooms myself, I'm so paranoid I'll leave something behind."

I grinned. "I'm the same way. Well, you have safe travels, you hear? Come back and visit us someday."

"I'd like that. There's still a lot to explore."

I left her and continued down the hall. The next room was Sarah's. Her door had been open when I first came up the hall, but now was closed.

Sarah was a strange one. Always in the shadows.

I tapped on the door.

"Come in," she called.

I cracked the door open. "It's me, Georgie."

"Oh, hi!" She smiled, looking up from a pile of clothing on the bed, half folded, half a mess.

"Can I do anything to help?" I asked.

"I don't know what, but come on in. And shut the door."

I shut it and headed to the bed. "You want help folding these?"

"Sure. I'm not particular."

I lifted a t-shirt and shook it. "Very cute."

She smiled. "It's nice to get a chance to wear casual clothes."

"Oh? You don't normally? What do you do back in the real world?"

"I work at..." She hesitated. "I mean, I'm unemployed right now."

Unemployed? Who takes a vacation when they're unemployed? I folded another t-shirt. "Aw, that's too bad. Was it recent? I'm sorry."

"Yeah, I'm out there now shilling my résumé, attending job fairs, that sort of thing."

"What kind of job are you applying for?"

She shrugged. "Something completely different from my last job. I'm kind of looking to get into a new field. Something fresh. You know, I teach kickboxing right now at the Y. Maybe I'll get into something more like that."

I nodded. "I get it. My last job was demanding with long hours. I loved it, but it *was* nice to get out of that."

"Yeah. So you understand stressful jobs. Mine was like that. To top it off, I had a boss that I couldn't stand, and.... Sometimes you can only get pushed so far." Her lips pressed together. She balled a fist and slammed it into the mattress, making her rather impressive bicep flex. Suddenly, the memory of the dagger in Mr. Green's chest came to mind. I swallowed.

Sarah got up and walked over to her suitcase and heaved it onto the bed. The bed dipped under its weight.

I raised an eyebrow. "Wow. That looks heavy."

She grinned. "It is."

"You need help getting it down the stairs?" I asked.

Sarah flexed her arm a few times and gave me a wry grin. "Nah. I think I've got it covered."

I smiled, trying to hide the growing feeling of alarm. "Well, I hope you find a nice calm job when you get back. You might need it after everything that's happened the last few days. You think you'll stay in contact with anyone here?"

"Like who?" she asked with a chuckle.

Good point. "It seemed like you got along with the St. Claires."

"They're nice. We'll see."

"How about Mrs. Green?"

"This is terrible, but I'm not sure how I feel about her."

"Was it because Eliza Sue confronted Mr. Peterson for sneaking around with Rachel?" I asked.

Sarah's look was intentionally casual. "She just came off very fake. Though I was surprised at the news it was Rachel cheating. If anyone were committing infidelity, I'd have expected it to be Mr. Green."

My eyebrows flew up. "Whoa! What?"

"I heard him talking one day. He must have been outside on a walk."

"Where were you?" I asked.

Sarah smiled. "I was inside the shed." She licked her lip and her smile got bigger. "With Mr. Peterson."

"Oh, my," I said, shaking my head. I kind of had a feeling.

"We were just having a bit of fun." She shrugged. "The attraction's fizzled out now. Anyway, we heard them talking."

I felt like my brain was trying to catch up with the information she was giving. I erased the thought of her and Mr. Peterson canoodling. "Who's them?"

CHAPTER 25

"What did you hear?" I asked Sarah again.

"It was muffled. Mr. Green was talking to someone. Maybe he was even on his phone. It sounded like he said that they were safe, no one knew. That, in just a few days, they'd be free. They could start over anywhere in the world."

"Did you tell anyone this?" I asked. Dread balled in the pit of my stomach.

"No. I mean, why would I? I didn't see who he was talking to. Besides, Mr. Peterson was being quite distracting." She grinned again. "Maybe I heard it all wrong."

My mind was spinning, and I didn't like where it was going. Who was the other person Mr. Green was referring too? Was it Mrs. Green? Someone else? I wished Sheriff Parker hadn't said everyone could leave today.

I finished folding the pants I'd been holding and then set them in a pile. I stood up. "I'm just going to check on everyone else, okay? If you need anything, call me."

"You got it. You've been an excellent host. Maybe I'll come back another year to finish the tour."

I shot her a fake grin, hoping I'd never see any of these people again. At least not for a long, long while. "You do that."

Her phone rang at that moment. She leaned over to retrieve it from the bedside table.

"Hello?" she answered.

I started to head out to give her privacy when I heard her say, "Thank you, Sheriff Parker." Her next comment was directed to me as I opened the door. "Guess what? We're all free to leave. I'll be out of your hair in ten minutes."

My stomach sank at her words, but I shot her a thumbs-up. If Sheriff Parker didn't see a reason to keep them here, then who was I to think I knew better?

I shut the door and headed downstairs to check on the St. Claires. Their door was shut, and they didn't respond to my gentle tapping.

I walked into the kitchen. For the first time, Cecelia wasn't there. I peered out the window and saw her standing in her garden with a rake and flowered work gloves on. I smiled at the sight. Darn it all, if I didn't want to be as active as she was at that age.

The St. Claires emerged from their room. Mr. St. Claire dragged two suitcases. "Well, it's been fun, but we're out of here," he announced.

Mrs. St. Claire flipped her red hair off her shoulder. "It's been an adventure, to say the least. An anniversary I'll never forget. I can't wait to get back home to talk about it."

"You two travel safely," I said as I waved goodbye.

It wasn't long before the rest of the guests had trundled through the doorway with their bags. I bid them all the same thing, and it was with the biggest sigh of relief when the front door closed for the final time.

I glanced out the back window again. Poor Cecelia had missed the goodbyes, but she had a smile on her face as she continued to winterize her garden. I left the kitchen to start flipping the rooms, and get things prepared for next week's guests.

Cecelia came in eventually to help me. Her voice had been casual when she noted the guests were gone. I suspected her timing in the garden was intentional. She'd probably been just as ready to be done with the group as I was.

I was exhausted from the stripping and remaking of the beds, and cleaning the bathrooms and floors. It was dark by the time we finished. We didn't find anything else, which was a good thing. I'd send the box to Mrs. Green tomorrow.

Cecelia did find the window screen, though. Oddly enough, it was tucked under the bed of the empty room. Mr. Peterson must have snuck in here, removed the screen, and climbed down the tree, later returning the same way.

Something about that scenario bothered me, but I was too tired to puzzle it out. Cecelia sent me home with a couple of sandwiches, and made me promise her that I'd take my vitamins.

Even though it was already dark out, I took another drive before heading home. Not as far as the other day, but I needed time to clear my head. A mental palate cleanser, so to speak.

But this time, I never got that feeling of peace. No, my mind was at unrest, nagged by something I couldn't quite put my finger on. I finally gave up and drove to the hospital.

That ended up being a bust. Since I wasn't family, and Leslie still was admitted to the ICU, they weren't free to give me any information. I assumed that meant she still wasn't conscious. With a heavy heart, I returned home.

I walked into the apartment, flipped on the lamp, and then settled in front of the TV with my sandwiches and some hot cocoa to veg out.

It was late by the time I was thinking I should probably try to sleep. The uneasy feeling had grown inside me despite being treated to trash TV and sugar.

I opened my computer in one last attempt to figure out what my problem was before I went to bed.

First, I searched for Mr. Green's company. The news sites shouted the same thing Frank had told me earlier. The business was under investigation for pilfering away the retirees' fund, and now was going bankrupt.

Has to be enemies there, I thought. *I wonder if any of the guests were affected by the stolen pension fund?*

One by one, I searched the guests' names.

Mr. St. Claire came up as a real estate broker in Michigan.

Mrs. St. Claire had no job history. I'm not ashamed to say I scanned her Facebook. Most of her posts were about how fabulous her life was, and I caught more than a hint of exaggeration. I paused at one post where she shared that she'd recently quit smoking. It made me wonder how successful it had been, and if that red-lipsticked butt had been from her sneaking out one night.

David Peterson showed up as a smiling salesman at a used car lot. One that got horrible reviews, according to the Better Business Bureau.

And I realized Peterson and Mr. St. Claire most likely did have a run-in with each other, despite Mr. St. Claire's denial. Though no charges had been filed, about ten years ago they'd both been mentioned in the New York Daily in conjecture to a gambling ring in Brooklyn. I remembered the nastiness that had flown around the table while they played cards. It was easy to see there was real bad blood there.

Eliza Sue showed up as a personal assistant in a conglomerate. She also apparently volunteered at the library.

Sarah's name came up as the winner of an amateur bodybuilding event, along with working as a day trader on the stock market.

Mrs. Green had her name linked as the host of several charity luncheon events, along with an enormous write-up a year ago on a gossip site detailing her wedding.

But nothing gave me any solid evidence for a real suspect. I thought about giving up, but another idea occurred to me. Odd. Weird. Probably brought on by the third cup of hot cocoa and sleeplessness.

I logged into the genealogy site. On another page, I brought up the article on the Three Maidens' Manor. After finding the full names of the soldiers killed, I started my search of family trees.

It was an hour of work. Just one hour. But I had an answer. I knew who killed Mr. Green. And I realized all the clues had pointed to this person all along.

Excitement tingled my skin as I reached for the phone. I stopped when I saw the time. It was nearly two in the morning. I remembered Frank's cough and sweaty appearance, and I realized I couldn't call. I didn't know what was going on with him, but he needed his sleep. And all I had was conjecture, really. I sent him a text to call me first thing in the morning, along with the name of who I thought had murdered Mr. Green.

Weariness really weighed on me as I brought my dishes into the kitchen. I stared at the bottle of pills. Was tonight the night to stop?

My head was shaking in the negative before the question was fully asked. No, I couldn't face the monsters tonight. I shook a pill out and swallowed it with the last of the hot cocoa.

Ten minutes later, I was asleep in bed.

WHAT WAS THAT? My eyes opened and I strained to see into the darkness. My mind was groggy in the way it was when I hadn't fully slept off the effects of the pill yet.

Did I just hear what I thought I'd heard? Was I dreaming?

There it was again. Soft shuffling. I sat straight up in bed, my heart pounding.

A brilliant light flashed in my face. My hands flew up to shield my eyes. Adrenaline raced through my body. *This is real! This is really happening.* My legs trembled under the blankets.

"Where is it?" A low voice hissed. My mind registered another level of shock.

"Wh-what?"

The light left as whoever it was flashed it around the room. I blinked as my eyes struggled to adjust.

I struggled to make out details.

Bam! The light hit my eyes again. I squinted and ducked my head. I was scared to shield my eyes, afraid I wouldn't see the person coming closer. I wiped them as they watered.

"How did you get in here?" I asked.

I should have known better. The pistol shining in the light made me shut up pretty quick.

"I'll ask you one more time. Where is it?" The voice was steady. Cold.

I knew who it was. The killer. I'd thought all the guests had gone home, and I was safe to wait until morning. I mentally kicked myself for allowing myself to get into this place. And it stung twice as bad that it was me who'd given them the code into the building in the first place.

CHAPTER 26

They say that when you're about to die, your entire life flashes before your eyes. Well, I don't know about that. But what did flash before my eyes were regrets.

A lot of them.

Why had I lived like I had limitless time? Why didn't I pursue my dreams *now*, instead of putting them off for a future that was never promised to me? Why did I let the past dictate whether I would be happy or successful today?

And most of all, why didn't I take the time to face the pain, and then allow myself a life unshackled by it?

Why? Why? Why?

The regret was real. It was huge. It was so big that it was

almost worse than the fear from staring down the barrel of a gun.

I squinted and tried to peer through the fingers of my blocking hand. "Eliza Sue?"

She sighed. "Honestly, I'm about done with all of this. Just give me the book."

"I ... I don't have it," I answered, kicking myself again for telling her that it was at my place. But what if I hadn't? Would Cecelia be facing this gun instead?

"What do you mean, you don't have it?" she asked, her voice tinged with impatience.

"The police. They have it." My voice was high with fear.

The barrel of the gun wavered. "Well, that's not good news for you then, is it?" she asked.

"You should run," I said. "Make your escape now and go into hiding. The cops... they know it's you."

She laughed. "How do they know it's me? Everything's gone perfectly."

"Except for you getting caught with the book. You said that you double-triple checked hotel rooms, afraid to leave something behind. You checked the Green's room and got caught by Sarah."

She tutted her tongue in disapproval. "I had to check, just in case. The dumb man left it under his pillow. He wasn't supposed to bring it with him."

"You knew the book led to something?"

"He told me his family history years ago, about ten years after I started working for him. He trusted me. How there'd been a treasure buried. He knew his family had once lived in Pennsylvania, but he didn't know where. His ancestors cut all ties to the three women once the war was over, trying to carve a new life. One that didn't end with a rope around their necks for treason. He showed me the book one day, and I was immediately intrigued by the dedication and the drawing."

She took a deep breath and continued. "I did a search for the poem, and the original first line showed up. When I searched for three maids, the line the penciled drawing pointed to, the manor was the first thing on the browser list. I knew this was it. And your bed and breakfast site was next on the search site, boasting of a tour of the place. The plan practically formed itself."

"So you printed an invitation to give him?"

She shifted and the bed jiggled. I realized she was sitting at the end. "I made it for Michael to give his new wife. As an excuse to get down here. Once I informed him that I thought I'd found the treasure, he was on board."

"And you came along because...? Were you having an affair?"

She growled in anger, making me flinch. "Absolutely not! I told him he might need help. His plan was to find the treasure and leave the country. He knew the audit against his company was going to uncover a lot of dirt."

"Why didn't you just steal the treasure when you broke in the night before to tamper with the lamp?"

"Quite honestly, neither of us knew what to look for. But Michael's family legend said he'd recognize it when he saw it. So I had to trust that he would find it. According to the bottom of the poem, he knew it had something to do with butcher, baker, or candlestick maker."

"When did you find out what it was?" I asked.

"When I caught him holding it in his hand. During his bathroom trip."

"The same time you left for the bathroom, too."

"Yes," she chuckled. "Then."

"It was the candelabra," I suggested, hoping I was right.

"It was. When he saw the candelabra, he knew that was where it was. Because he had the same one at home. During the siege of Three Maidens', Elizabeth Hartwell unscrewed the base of the brass candlestick and placed her family's jewels inside."

"So why not steal it from him later? Why sabotage the lamp at all?"

"You know why." Her voice held humor in it. Sick humor.

"Leslie whispered it. To get revenge."

She laughed. "How did you find out?"

"I started seeing you had your finger in a lot of pies, as Cecelia would say. It was you who planted the idea that Mr. Peterson had lost a button. You must have noticed you were missing one. Very subtle. Good job."

She didn't answer, so I continued. "But the problem with saying that you fixed his shirt was that it didn't make sense why you would help him, not after your accusations of him cheating with Rachel. You'd been so disgusted. I knew that integrity was important to you by the way you talked about teachers. The longer I thought about it, the more I wondered if you were *really* helping him."

"Used car salesman sleaze," she growled. "Scum of the earth."

She still had the gun. I wasn't about to argue. During this entire time, my mind had been spinning nearly out of control trying to figure out how to both appease her and escape. I slowly felt for my pepper spray. Where was it?

"Please continue. The story is just getting interesting," she said. Moonlight from the window glinted off the barrel of the gun.

I cleared my throat. "Well, I got to thinking, the only one who said they'd seen Mr. Peterson and Mrs. Green cheating *was* you. The other supposed witness, Mr. Green, obviously couldn't contest the story. Everyone knew Mr. Peterson was a flirt and a player, so it was believable. You popped out the screen in the upstairs empty bedroom to support your story. And then there was the anonymous tip the police received about Mr. Peterson meeting with Mrs. Green back in Brooklyn. You gave them that. You set up Mr. Peterson to take the fall for the murder by providing the motive of love."

"You're starting to bore me," she said with a fake yawn.

Panic zipped through me. What was I going to do when my story ran out? I swallowed hard and tried to control my breathing. "You were the one that floated around the gossip that Mrs. Green is pregnant."

"She probably is. I did actually see her with that sleaze-ball Peterson."

"Was it her, or Sarah?"

"One or the other. Both are tramps. Does it really make a difference?"

Again, I wasn't going to argue.

"Anything else?" she asked.

"The paper bag with the metal water bottle in it. The water bottle was huge, and you insisted on bringing it. That's how you got the dagger into the house. You volunteer at the library and said that you love to study history and non-fiction. You learned where the best place was to stab someone."

"Took some practice stabbing roasts at home to get the angle and the strength right, but I think I did a good job."

"I get why you used the dagger, but why the wheat penny?"

She smiled. "That was something subtle, something just for me. The wheat penny was the first coin to have a human likeness on it, Abraham Lincoln. It was minted one hundred years after Abraham's birth, in 1809. A very important year to me."

"1809?" I eased my pepper spray out from under the pillow, praying she was distracted by her own cleverness.

"Have I stumped you, Miss Know-it-all? Can't you answer the million-dollar question? Do you know why that year matters? Why I did all of this?"

"You are a descendent of Captain Heyward."

"Yes, I am. Very clever girl. Very clever. In 1809, Captain

Heyward's uncle, Thomas Heyward Jr., signer of the United States Declaration of Independence that heralded the American Revolution, died. I thought using the wheat penny was quite fitting."

"For revenge for a two-hundred-year-old murder?"

"The Greens and their ancestors were murderers and thieves. Even the jewels had been stolen from somebody or other. They'd always been criminals and, as the stolen retiree fund proved, they still were. It was time to right some wrongs. I was able to take out an old family enemy and all around bad guy, and steal their treasure while I was at it. And I succeeded."

"You did." I agreed. "So why did you go back to the Three Maidens'?" I eased off the safety mechanism of the spray.

"I'd been waiting for the perfect time to get the candelabra. Obviously, I couldn't trot out with it that night. I overheard you on the phone with that curator lady, and thought you both were meeting somewhere for lunch. It was too bad for her that wasn't the case."

My heart thumped in my throat. I was at the end of the story. I'd run out of time. It was now or never. I eyed the gun, still pointed at me.

Would this thing spray if I didn't shake it? I had no choice. I was about to find out.

I thought of Derek. If I lived or died, one way or another, I was going to face what happened that night.

One. Two. Three.

I dove to my side while bringing my arm out from under the covers. I depressed the trigger and a cloud of chemicals came out.

The gun went off. Everything went red.

I screamed.

Derek.

CHAPTER 27

he red haze grew and my eyes burned. I couldn't see anymore, but just kept depressing the trigger of the pepper spray. By the sound, I could tell it was empty. I threw it at her and rolled off the side of the bed.

Tears streamed down my face. I wiped my eyes with the edge of the sheet. I could hear her flailing about and coughing. She was screaming. Cursing. The gun went off again, and I heard the bullet hit the mattress where I'd just been. My ears ringing, I struck out for my phone on the nightstand. I grabbed it, nearly sobbing with relief. I couldn't see to dial and hit the last number called, praying someone would answer.

"Hello?" Frank's voice came through the receiver. I threw the phone on the bed, too scared to answer to give her a reason to pinpoint where I was.

She was still coughing violently. I chanced a peek and saw her doubled over.

"Georgie?" Frank yelled from the bed.

Eliza Sue choked as she tried to respond in a string of angry words. I nearly jumped up to try and knock her down. But then she turned the gun toward the phone and fired.

The sound was deafening.

"Where are you?" she screamed.

I squatted beside the bed, ready to spring. I had to get to her and get the gun before she recovered. I thought of Derek again and jumped forward.

She was heavier than me. But she didn't see me coming. I concentrated all my weight on the arm that held the gun. I landed a blow on her forearm's soft muscle, causing the pistol to fly away. It landed close to us. I couldn't let her get it again.

Her fingers came like claws for my face. I shoved them away, but not before her nails caught my cheek. She tried to force her eyes open, but the chemicals were too strong.

Now that I was next to her, it was affecting me more too. I started coughing harder, my eyes tearing up even more. My nose was running. The skin where she clawed me burned like fire.

We wrestled on the floor. My only goal was to keep her away from the gun. I had to reach it first.

She was strong, stronger than I realized. Slowly, she maneuvered me to my back, trying to reach for my throat. I reached for the pistol with my foot, but only pushed it farther away.

I could do this. I knew I could. I wasn't going to let her win. My muscles flamed with fatigue.

But she was getting tired, too. I could feel it in her movements, clumsier, less deliberate. I just had to wait her out.

She shrieked in frustration and I knew my moment was here. Lifting my arm up, I did a quick hip roll that knocked her off. I lunged for the gun.

"Stop!" I shouted, my hands on the weapon. "Don't move."

She sat back, panting, wheezing, still coughing. Her eyes struggled to focus on me and saw the pistol. With a groan, she fell back against the floor.

I wiped at my face and looked for the phone to call the police.

A bullet hole had shattered the front screen. I wasn't calling anyone.

As best as I could, I kept my watering eyes on her and backed up toward the door. If nothing else, I'd scream for help in the hallway. The neighbors had to have heard this.

I'd just made it into the kitchen when my front door crashed open. Frank was there, gun out. His eyes were wild and crazy when he saw me.

"Georgie!" He started toward me.

"No! Don't!" I coughed some more and then pointed into the living room. His gaze caught sight of my pistol. With his hand, he waved to direct me to put the gun down. Then he maneuvered around the corner, making a quick head check to make sure it was clear.

"Police!" he yelled. I heard a tackling sound and winced. Wearily, I peered around the corner. He was on top of her, handcuffing her hands behind her back. He was already sniffling.

After a minute, he returned to the kitchen. Now his coughing started in earnest. "Pepper spray, Georgie?" he asked between coughs.

"Now you know I was prepared. And how on earth did you have your handcuffs on you at this time of night? What were you using them for, hmm?" I asked, trying to interject some humor.

"They're a part of my belt. I grabbed it when I heard the gunshot over the phone. The rest of the cavalry should be here any minute." He stared at me with one eye squeezed closed.

We walked out into the hallway for fresh air. Mrs. Costello's door opened.

"Everything's okay, but stay in your apartment," Frank said, his voice deepening to his "official police business" tone.

Mrs. Costello didn't seem to believe him.

"It's okay," I said. "The police are on their way."

She gave him a distrustful frown before shutting her door.

"You okay, Georgie?" he asked. His finger reached toward my cheek. He froze millimeters from touching me. His eyes caught mine, and I saw real fear there.

I couldn't answer. My eyes welled up a bit, not because of any irritant, but because I was touched by his caring. I nodded and tried to smile.

The front door crashed open downstairs. His gaze swept in that direction. "And the cavalry is here."

They came thundering up the stairs. It was a chaotic few

minutes as they tried to figure out who we were and what was going on. But soon, they had Eliza Sue in custody.

———

It was a long night of giving statements—more statements! I was getting to be a pro—propped up by a few cups of coffee. Frank was a trooper; I never thought I'd say that. He stuck around the entire time.

Finally, hours of shivering in the hallway later, they allowed me back into my house. The sun was just coming up over the horizon, filling my home with soft gray light. I rubbed my arms. It was cold as heck in here. Someone had set fans in the open windows to circulate fresh air.

I wandered into the bedroom, and ruefully grinned at the bullet holes the police had circled with paint. One bullet had smashed into the phone, which they collected for evidence. The other had been dug out of the four-by-four that made up the headboard of my bed.

The final one was somewhere in the mattress, presumably lost forever. It was this bullet hole that I was studying now. Nothing remarkable, just a small hole burned into the top of the mattress covering. But one that could have killed me since it was right where I'd been laying.

I sat on the bed and sighed. I couldn't help myself, and put my pinky in the bullet hole.

"They can't get it out," Frank said from where he was leaning against the doorjamb.

I lifted my head, surprised he'd followed me in, and then nodded.

"Kind of like me." He tapped his chest. "I've got some shrapnel in here that still causes me trouble. Doctors can't get it though."

"I'm sorry, Frank." I meant it. He was only thirty-two. We'd grown up together, two bratty kids throwing snowballs at each other and trying to get the other in trouble. As much as he always drove me crazy, it hurt my heart to see him hobbled by pain.

"I'm a tough old bird. You know that." His face broke into a grin. "And you are too, Georgie. You are, too."

I rolled my eyes. "I don't know if I'm more insulted that you called me old, or a bird."

He laughed then, and I did, too. Then, I started the conversation again, a little more serious. "Is the shrapnel why you've been a little off lately? The coughing and stuff?"

He rubbed his chest. "Yeah. It gets me in the winter. Doctors say the scar tissue will protect me soon enough, but it's been two years. Still waiting, I guess. It makes it hard to sleep at night."

I glanced down. "I have a hard time sleeping, too."

He didn't respond to that, and I didn't say anything more, either. The seconds of silence between us grew.

But this time, I was okay. I was okay with letting my guard down, and leaving that tiny window to my vulnerability open. I was ready to face things. Maybe not all at once, but I wasn't going to hide from what happened on that night any longer. I might have to go to a counselor to get things sorted out, but it was time for me to do that.

Frank cleared his throat and took a step toward me. Something was in his hand. He lifted it up. "Here. I guess I owed ya."

It was a soda.

I smiled as I took it. He smiled too, and shoved his hands in his pockets. "Glad you're back, kid."

I popped the tab and gave him a cheers in return, then took a long drink, snorting slightly at the sharp taste of bubbles so early in the morning. I *was* back, with a new chance at life.

No more car rides to hide from the memories.

I owed Derek that.

And I owed myself that freedom, too.

The End

Thank you for reading Cherry Pie or Die. Hope you enjoyed Georgie's journey as she tries to get back on her feet. Here is the link to book two, Cookies and Scream.

Here are her first two recipes.

Georgie's rainyday-I'm-just-going-to-try-this-baking-gig-Cherry Crisp

1 can (21 ounce) cherry pie filling

3/4 cup flour

3/4 cup rolled oats

2/3 cup dark brown sugar

3/4 tsp cinnamon

1 1/2 sticks softened butter

Directions

Preheat oven to 350 degrees F (175 degrees C.) Lightly grease a 2 quart baking dish. Open pie filling and spread it evenly in the dish.

In a separate bowl, mix together flour, oats, sugar, cinnamon, and nutmeg. Cut in the soft butter with a fork and knife. You can also use your fingers. Don't over mix- you want it to stay in large crumbles.

Sprinkle on top of the cherry filling.

Bake in the preheated oven for 30 minutes, or until topping is golden brown.

Aunt Cecelia's Cherry Pie-so-good-it'll-make-you-cry

First make pastry for crust and refrigerate for at least thirty minutes.

Preheat oven to 400degrees F (220 C).

Filling-

1 1/2 tablespoons softened butter, to dot

1 cup sugar

2 tablespoons separated sugar to use at end.

2 tablespoons cornstarch

1/4 teaspoon salt

2 (14 1/2 ounce) cans pitted tart cherries, drained, reserving 1/2 cup of the juice

1/4 teaspoon almond extract

2 teaspoons lemon juice

1/2 tsp vanilla

1 pastry for a double-crust 9-inch pie

1 egg (yolk separated and saved for egg wash)

Drain cherries, reserving 1/2 cup liquid. In a small bowl, combine sugar, cornstarch and salt. In a separate medium-sized bowl, combine cherry juice, almond extract, vanilla and lemon juice. Add the dry ingredients and mix well.

Add cherries and mix well again. Let it sit for fifteen minutes.

On lightly covered surface, roll out half of the pastry into an 11 inch circle. Place into 9 inch pie dish. Trim overhanging edges.

Roll other half of pastry into another 11 inch circle. With a knife or pastry wheel, cut ten 3/4-inch-wide strips.

Wider strips are easier to weave together.

Pour cherry mixture into pie crust. Dot with butter. Finish top with weaving lattice with pie crust. Lightly brush lattice with egg yolk and sprinkle with remaining two tablespoons of sugar.

Bake for 50 minutes.

Pastry recipe

1 1/2 sticks very cold unsalted butter

2 3/4 cups all-purpose flour

1 teaspoon salt

1 tablespoon sugar

1/2 cup ice water

Combine flour, salt, and sugar. Pour into a mixer or food processor. Cut butter and add, mixing until mixture resembles coarse meal. Sprinkle with 1/4 cup ice water. Mix until dough is mixed to pea-sized crumbles but holds together when squeezed. If needed, add more water one tablespoon at a time, until the dough reaches that consistency. Don't over mix.

Divide into two balls and then flatten into disks and wrap in plastic. Refrigerate at least 30 minutes.

Enjoy! Here is the next in the Baker Street Cozy Mystery series! Read the entire series free with Kindle Unlimited.

Cookies and Scream

Made in the USA
San Bernardino, CA
05 June 2020